HYWEL'S ⌐R

Elinor Wyatt

ABEREIFED BOOKS

HYWEL'S WINTER

All Rights Reserved

0-9545781-0-4

First Published 2003 by
Abereifed Books, Llechryd, Cardigan, SA43 2QN
www.abereifed.co.uk

Printed in Great Britain for Abereifed Books

HYWEL'S WINTER

TO GLYNNE

MAIN CHARACTERS

Anwyl	King's nephew
Aulus	Roman general
Bear	Gwent warrior
Bedwyr	Duach's father
Camlach	Champion warrior
Caradog	King's grandson
Cathmor	Irish warrior
Cei	Duach's friend
Dewi	Roman ex-tribune
Duach	Hywel's best friend
Elen	Hywel's stepmother
Emrys	Bard
Gryffydd	Owain's sailing master
Gwain	Lord of Emlyn
Hafgan	Minor chief
Huw	Lord Modron's son
Hywel	14 year old son of Owain
Iolo	Hywel's groom
Lucius	Aulus' personal slave
Mabon	High druid
Mellt	Hywel's horse
Modron	Lord of Daugleddef
Owain	Hywel's father
Pebyn	Hywel's enemy
Rhiannon	Hywel's grandmother
Rhys	Lord of Cemais
Tegwyn	Owain's brother
Tewdwr	Tegwyn's son

CANTREFS OF DYFED

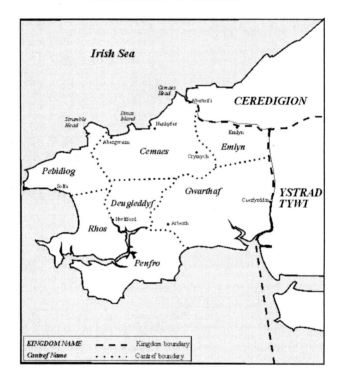

Irish Sea

Cemaes Head

Aberteifi

CEREDIGION

Strumble Head

Dinas Bland

Hanhyfer

Abergwain

Cemaes

Emlyn

Emlyn

Crymych

Pebidiog

Solfa

Gwarthaf

Caerfyrddin

YSTRAD TYWI

Deugleddyf

Hwlfford

Arberth

Rhos

Penfro

| KINGDOM NAME | – – – | Kingdom boundary |
| Cantref Name | · · · · · | Cantref boundary |

CHAPTER 1 – THE FINAL TEST

It is strange how starvation makes your hearing keener, thought Hywel, as he picked up the faint sound of horsemen in the distance; three or four of them coming slowly. Time for another couple of handfuls of blackberries before he needed to get into hiding. A kilometre from his target was no place to get captured after all he had been through!

He took his plunder and wriggled into the centre of a coppiced hazel bush that gave plenty of cover and a good view of the forest track. The four horsemen were riding at their ease and two of them were talking cheerfully. The others, who looked like grooms, trailed silently at a respectful distance. No threat there, he thought, as he sucked the juice out of particularly luscious blackberry.

Then he nearly died of shock! The leading rider was Pebyn - Pebyn who had tried to kill him four years before and had been banished by High Druid Mabon. It couldn't be! But it was! Sloppy, slimy, stupid Pebyn. He had not changed much. He had grown a bit but he was still fat, pasty, and unhealthy-looking; he still slouched on his horse; and he still looked like a sack of fir cones tied loosely round the middle. Why had Druid Mabon let him come back? And who was his companion?

Hywel watched them out of sight and then put them out of his mind. He would deal with them later; right now he had more important things to think about.

He was in the final stage of his tribe's warrior test. The test is the last, and worst, of a series of trials that start when boys are ten and finish around their fourteenth birthday. Then everyone legally becomes a man but only those who successfully complete the tough warrior training and tests become full warriors of the tribe. All the men of Hywel's family had been warriors since time before time and he certainly was not going to be the first one to fail - he couldn't bear the shame. In fact, he planned to do better than that. He was going to be the first of his year group to complete this test. That would make him the junior champion warrior of the cantref - which would be one in the eye for his friend Gwyn who was sure that the title was his.

He did not have long to wait now, just until dark. The harvest moon was going to be as much a problem tonight as it had been a help during the last three nights while he made his way across forty kilometres of rough country, hunted, with a price on his head. He had been abandoned blindfolded and naked, except for a wooden token on a thong around his neck, with instructions to make his way undetected back to the village of Nanhyfer within four days. He had also sworn an oath not to enter a building, not to accept help from anyone and not to steal food. The first two promises had been easy enough to keep but the last one was something else! Nuts and berries were not very filling and he was starving. Now there was only one problem left - getting across a bare field to touch a stake before a guard stopped him.

He got to the edge of the field just after dusk. While he was waiting for the right time to move, he heard a sleepy bleat from a sheep pen about fifty metres to his right. Sheep - the perfect diversion! He slithered across to them, grateful that there was no dog, loosened a hurdle and tried to persuade them to move out across the field so that he could hide behind them. The stupid animals just looked at him and refused to do anything.

One did get to its feet but moved to the back of the pen and then it lay down again. Goodbye diversion.

Hywel went back to watching the sentry. He walked past about ten metres in front of Hywel's bush, quietly humming a tune to himself. Hywel let him get well down the field and past the stake so that he would not be able to see movement out of the corner of his eye as Hywel made his attack.

Now! He got to his feet and moved steadily and smoothly towards the stake, trying to avoid the jerky and sudden movements that are so obvious at night. He was within two paces of it when the sentry saw him. Hywel dived and threw his arms around it as the sentry raised his spear.

"Halt! Lie on your face! Identify yourself!" he commanded.

"Hywel ap Owain."

"Your grandfather's name?"

"Meredith."

The sentry crossed the field and poked Hywel with the butt of his spear.

"You're the first one back, Hywel ap Owain ap Meredith, and that makes you the junior champion. Well done!"

Hywel buried his head in his arms and closed his eyes for a moment to hide his tears of relief. He had done it!

"On your feet!" commanded the sentry. Hywel used the stake to pull himself upright and grinned at him in delight. "Give me your token and take this one instead. Give it to the guard at the llys and he'll fix you up with food, clothes and a bed. But you'd better clean yourself up first - you stink like a pig."

"Thank you, sir," said Hywel, almost too excited to get the words out.

"Hywel!" he said sternly.

"Yes, sir?"

"Hywel, you idiot! Don't you realise? You're a man now and a warrior. You don't have to call me 'sir' any more."

Hywel's jaw dropped and he stared at the sentry for a long moment.

"So I don't," he said wonderingly. "It's a strange feeling. ... I suppose I'll get used to it sometime. Thank you and goodnight, ... Illtyd."

Hywel checked that the hurdle he had moved in the sheep pen was secure, washed himself in the river and made his way up to the llys.

Lord Rhys had established his llys on the site of an ancient hill fort and he had extended its defences over the top of three steep-sided hills to protect his own accommodation and the buildings necessary for the administration of the cantref as a whole. It was also the main base and barracks of the cantref war bands.

The footpath up to its main gate climbed the hill in a series of muscle-wrenching zigzags. Hywel felt really tired now that all the excitement was over and his legs were rubbery as he climbed up the stretch to the gate. He was swaying as he identified himself to the sentry and presented his new token. The guard commander gave him a mixed welcome.

"Well done, Hywel. Congratulations on being back first even though you've cost me two silver pieces. I bet on your friend Gwyn and I also bet that no-one would make it before midnight." Hywel just grinned at him through his tiredness. "Well, your clothes are in that hut over there. Grab a bowl and a spoon when you're dressed and help yourself to stew."

Hywel was in a daze as he clambered into the trews that were the sign of his new status and then pulled his tunic over his head. Both garments were itchy on his skin and he felt hot and uncomfortable as he started to spoon the lamb stew into his bowl. He dunked a big piece of bread into the stew and started to chew with enthusiasm. It was great! He didn't remember finishing the meal nor falling asleep on a pallet - everything just disappeared into a black void.

He woke late in the morning in a fizzing wave of excitement and looked around him cautiously. The hut was empty except for three of his friends. Duach, his best friend, was snoring softly but Gwyn and Twm were lying as dead. Someone had been thoughtful and the makings of a good breakfast sat waiting on a table. He collected a selection and went out into the sunlight where he found Illtyd having a late breakfast after his overnight sentry duty.

"Good morning, Hywel. Sleep all right?"

"Like the proverbial log, thank you, sir … sorry, … Illtyd. What happens now?"

"You eat your breakfast."

"Yes, of course. But I meant over this warrior business." Hywel grinned and started chewing.

"Well, nothing much until the other four get back - they have until midnight tonight. You might be able to go home in the meantime - that's up to Lord Pryderi. Then tomorrow warriors from all over the cantref gather here to help you swear the warrior's oath - we repeat ours at the same time - and then we watch you swear the oath of loyalty to Lord Rhys after which he gives you your swords. Then we have a monster feast when we try and make you drunk and then it's all over."

"Thank you. No-one had explained it before." Hywel finished his breakfast and sat quietly, thinking.

"Why so thoughtful, Hywel?" asked Illtyd.

"Well … everything's fine … but my father's still away on a trading voyage and he might not be back in time to see me get my sword, which would be a great pity."

Illtyd grinned broadly.

"He's with Lord Rhys at the moment and he's brought you a new horse. Look! Over there - it's a beauty, black as night."

"That's mine?"

"Yes - you lucky beast. I wish it were mine," he said with real longing in his voice. "Your father anchored two days ago so you'll have him and your uncle Tegwyn at the feast with you."

Hywel looked at him in astonishment.

"My father is here? In the llys? With Lord Rhys? And he brought me that horse? He was so sure that I'd make it?"

Illtyd nodded.

"That's right. Druid Mabon's here too. ... Hang on! You can't go rushing off to find him. You need permission from Lord Pryderi first. He's still in his own roundhouse. His baby isn't very well and he was up with him for most of the night."

The guard commander came up and collapsed onto the bench beside them.

"Wheww! I'm shattered! I'll be glad when we stop guarding that wretched stake - it doubles our work." He yawned hugely. "Lord Pryderi has given you all permission to go home when you wake up. Any sign of life from the others yet?"

"No, sir, they are all still pretty dead. Would you excuse me, please? My father is here and I'd like to find him if I can."

"Sit down! He left you a message - he'll come and meet you here when he's finished with Lord Rhys. ... Now, tell me Hywel, how on earth did you get back so much faster than everyone else and cause me to loose my bet? Gwyn has always won your year-group races and I was sure that he would win this one too. You didn't borrow a pony, did you?"

"No! Of course I didn't!"

"Joke! I didn't mean anything!"

"Well, ... you know the training we went through before the tests started?" He nodded. "I had been away on a ship all summer and I wasn't really fit - I wheezed like an old man when I tried to run up a hill. So, Edum ap Nislen, who was my tutor, arranged that should I take my meals at a farm on the next hill over, on the far side of a steep valley.

"He made me run up and down that valley, first once a day for my supper but, by the end of the fortnight, it was three times a day for my breakfast, lunch and supper - lunch was worst as the small hunk of bread and a mug of water wasn't worth the effort of fetching it - and it nearly killed me.

"If I took too long over any of the journeys, he made me chop wood at night before he let me go to sleep. All this on top of the normal weapons training! I hated him and, at one stage, I quite seriously considered killing him. But his system worked - and running over normal rough country during the test itself was child's play.

Poor Gwyn didn't stand a chance and he'll be terribly disappointed."

"That was evil of Edum. He's not supposed to torture you like that. He's supposed to be hard, but not brutal."

Hywel laughed.

"He wasn't on his own. Apparently, his father had trained mine, years ago, and my father had made him look an absolute fool. So he was paying off some old scores on me. I felt better when I realised that and I'll blackmail my father with it for ages."

"There's your father, coming now. Goodbye Hywel; well done."

CHAPTER 2 – THE JUNIOR CHAMPION

Hywel ran across to his father who was grinning from ear to ear. They saluted each other in Roman fashion and his father gave him the formal Latin greeting.

"Hail, Hywel son of Owain son of Meredith, junior champion of warriors!"

Hywel answered in the same way.

"Hail, Owain son of Meredith son of Tewdwr, father of warriors!"

Then, all of a sudden, Owain enveloped Hywel in a bear hug and shook him in delight.

"Hywel!" he said, as he held him at arm's length. "Hywel!"

"Yes, Father?"

"Hywel! You've grown, boy."

Hywel realised that he had, even in the two months that they had been apart. His father was less than half a handspan taller than him now. They were very alike: middle height; both sunburnt a dark brown; the same black, bushy hair; the same compact build; and they both moved in the same way - neatly, without wasting effort.

"Come and see your new horse, it's called Mellt - which means lightning. Tegwyn bought it for me from that breeder in Ceredigion and a groom came with it. I've also got a saddle for you; you are entitled to use one now that you are a man. It's a present from your Roman friend, Aulus Cornelius Calvus, in Gloucester. You would have been very touched to see how worried he was about you. He came the Roman general at me and told me precisely what he thought of our barbaric customs like warrior tests. He even told me that we deserved to be conquered by the Roman army so that they could be stamped out! I've got a lot to tell you about my trip, Aulus in particular - he's a very worried man - but that can wait until we are alone. Those two warriors are far too interested in us for us to talk secrets."

Hywel turned and saw that he was right. Illtyd and the guard commander were watching them closely and they waved when they saw that he had noticed them.

Owain chatted about unimportant things as he led Hywel across to the horse that was a magnificent stallion, a couple of hands taller than his current mare, and a glistening, glowing black all over. The horse shook its head at them and bared its teeth as they approached. Hywel made soothing noises until it let him touch it and then they started to make friends. Owain gave them a couple of minutes together before bringing the saddle across.

Hywel had never used a saddle before because boys had to ride barebacked and he was not sure how he was going to cope. Mellt did not seem to like saddles either and Hywel had quite a struggle getting it on him.

Then he did not seem to like Hywel and it took all his horsemanship to stay in his new saddle as they progressed down the path in a series of bucking jumps. Hywel stuck to him until they got down onto the flat at the foot of the hill and then Mellt really put on a virtuoso display that soon had Hywel flying through the air. Unforgivably, he also let go the reins and he expected to see his horse well on its way to the next cantref.

To Hywel's enormous surprise, Mellt walked over to him as he lay on the ground, winded and bruised, and first snuffled Hywel's face, then the rest of his body and then stood quietly until Hywel remounted.

"Oh dear, Hywel. You've got a problem," said his father, with real concern in his voice. "That horse is too intelligent. It was playing with you. You'll never master it. The best you can expect is to get it to agree to a partnership with you. If you can get that, then you've got something wonderful. If not, you're in trouble."

"We'll be friends, Father. We just need a bit of time to get to know each other. He'll be fine now. Tell me about your trip to Gloucester."

"No. I'm so proud of you. Tell me first about your training and the actual warrior test. Who did you draw as your tutor?"

Hywel laughed.

"You'll never believe it and I didn't want to. I nearly died when Lord Pryderi pulled the tokens out of the bag … I got Edum ap Nislen."

Owain groaned.

"Oh, no, Hywel. The gods couldn't have been so cruel."

"Oh, yes, Father. And they were! I had both father and son at me and, at one stage, I considered killing Edum but I didn't and I survived. But I reckon that I've already earned Mellt."

"I agree and I'll throw in a sword as well. … Edum and Nislen. … Poor Hywel."

"To give Edum his due - although he was vicious and unnecessarily cruel - he taught me well. I didn't collect a single fault during the weapons tests and I've never achieved that before. The cross-country test was easy. At a push, I could have made it back hours before I did but I went slowly and took care and I was still back well before all the others."

"Great! I got back in the middle of the pack when I took the test and Tegwyn was fool enough to tackle the stake in daylight when it was his turn. The sentry saw him, of course, and they were chasing each other round the field when his best friend nipped in and grabbed the stake first. Tegwyn was furious and they fought each other until the sentry threatened to disqualify them both. Tegwyn still lost and he's never forgiven his friend."

Mellt had been getting increasingly restless and difficult to handle as they rode at walking pace and he suddenly took off like a thunderbolt so Hywel only just caught his father's last words.

Mellt's first surge nearly unseated him but, after he collected himself and concentrated on what he was doing, Mellt gave him a marvellous ride. The horse was extremely sure-footed and seemed to flow over the ground with effortless power. Hywel shouted with delight and crouched low over its neck as it really started to run. They shot past the smith's house beside the bridge and then Mellt made a soaring leap from the path down onto the low-lying harvested hayfields where he lived up to his name and they flashed across them until they reached the outskirts of the village at Trefdraeth. Here he turned, almost without slackening his pace, splashed across the ford, and continued to gallop across the beach until he had circumnavigated it and got back to the ford. He then dropped to a trot and carried Hywel sedately up to his house on the ridge overlooking the village.

Owain was laughing and shaking his head in disbelief as they rode up to join him outside the front door of their house.

"And whose idea was that?" he demanded. "Yours or Mellt's?"

"Mellt's," said Hywel breathlessly. "I didn't do anything. I didn't give him any signals at all. He did it all by himself. Isn't he wonderful?"

He slid off his horse's back, rubbed its nose and patted it. Mellt tolerated it for a couple of moments and then started to move towards his stable.

Hywel let go the reins and watched him. He minced across the grass but stopped suddenly, just before he reached the hedge. Hywel's three-year-old twin brothers came hurtling round the hedge, almost immediately under his nose, with their cousin Tewdwr in hot pursuit. Tewdwr stopped and stared in wonder at Mellt and put out a tentative hand towards the reins. Mellt completely ignored him and stalked round the corner into the stable-yard.

"I just don't believe it!" laughed Owain. "Hywel, you're going to have to do something about that horse, and soon too, otherwise he'll take us over."

"Yes, indeed. I'll go right now. Would you apologise to Nan for me, please? I won't be long."

Hywel found a thin, freckled, intelligent-looking youngster of about twelve with his arms around Mellt's neck, whispering into his ear. He introduced himself shyly as Iolo ap Eliud.

"My... my father breeds horses, sir, up near Aberystwyth and I've looked after Mellt ever since he was born. I love him. I... I didn't want to be separated from him. I came here with him. Y... your uncle engaged me as a groom. He said that you would have to agree. P... p... please let me stay ... please."

His anxious eyes filled his face and tears welled as he waited for the answer.

Hywel grinned at him and punched him lightly on his arm.

"Of course you can stay, Iolo. I'm only too pleased to have you, particularly if you have any control over Mellt. I don't yet - he does just what he pleases with me!"

Iolo smiled shyly and took a deep, calming breath.

"You have to explain things to him first, sir. ... Then he's no problem. He doesn't like saddles much nor ... bridles. I did tell him that you needed them. ... I thought that he'd be good. Wasn't he?"

"No. We had an argument and he won. ... I'm afraid I can't stay with him now; I've got to go and see my grandmother. Could you tell him that I love him too and I'll be back later?"

"Yes, of course, sir."

The hall was crowded when Hywel went into the house and his stepmother, Elen, his uncles and his cousins made a tremendous fuss of him. His uncle Tegwyn seemed to have grown even wider since he had been away and his voice echoed round the rafters as he spluttered indignantly over Edum and Nislen.

Tegwyn's eldest son wanted to know all about the cross-country test, as he was eleven now and his own trial was not that far away.

Most of the female members of the family bustled about getting food and ale for the men under the direction of Elen, Hywel's stepmother.

Hywel's grandmother sat quietly, saying nothing, as the noise swirled round her. Eventually, the family got distracted and she moved out into her herb garden, making a small gesture for him to follow her.

"Well, Hywel? Are you still in one piece?" she asked with a smile as she sat on her favourite bench.

He flopped onto the grass at her side.

" Only just, Nan," he replied quietly.

"Was it that bad?"

"Worse. I've never been hated before. The druid's camp that I went to when I was ten was nasty and I was thankful when it finished. But there was nothing personal - they really wanted you to succeed. I'm still not sure if Nislen was trying to kill me to get back at my father. He made my life a real misery and, if I hadn't sworn an oath to obey his son, I would have run away. As I couldn't break my oath, I was determined that I wouldn't let Nislen break me - but it was hard. ... I will never ill-treat a slave or a servant again."

"You haven't done so yet, have you?"

"No, of course not! But I hadn't realised before how vulnerable they are."

"Well, young man. Try to put it all behind you if you can. I have a present here for you from your friend Tiernon, the Prince of Powys you rescued on your first voyage."

Hywel grinned and started tearing at the wrapping. Tiernon was as crazy as a coot but Hywel had spent a fantastic holiday with him a couple of years before and his memories were still vivid. Tiernon was still crazy thought Hywel as he gazed in awe at his present.

"Look, Nan," he whispered "isn't it fantastic?"

She examined the gold torc that he was holding out to her. The torc is the Celtic badge of manhood and they are made of a variety of metals and thicknesses to reflect their owner's status in the tribe - only warriors and nobles can wear gold ones.

Owain's is a gleaming, soft gold about three centimetres in diameter and beautifully ornamented. It is the traditional mark of the chief of his clan and it is very, very old.

"This is perfect, Hywel," said his grandmother. "It is just right for a brand new warrior without any money. Anything thicker would have been too showy and anything thinner would have been too mean. And look at the fantastic workmanship! It is a more than adequate gift for saving his life. When were you planning to visit him again?"

"I don't know, Nan. Perhaps sometime this winter except that the passes through the high mountains will be closed by snow from the middle of November to the end of February and that doesn't give me much time to fix it up."

"Well, do not worry about it now. Bard Emrys is coming to supper and we were both looking forward to you playing your flute tonight. He assured me that you would be back early. Apparently, he took a quick peek into your mind yesterday and found that you were very close to Nanhyfer."

"I'll kill him! I must have been too tired to block my mind against him - but I wish he wouldn't pry."

"I asked him to, Hywel. You hadn't contacted me for ages and I was worried."

Hywel had discovered at the druid's camp when he was ten that he shared, with Druid Mabon and Bard Emrys, the peculiar ability to read and influence minds. It was an enormous secret but his grandmother had known from the beginning. He normally talked to her every evening when he was away from her but this time he had been too miserable.

"Nan! I wish you wouldn't. ... But I forgive you."

"So you should! You're still small enough to go over my knee!"

He got to his feet and hugged her. He was quite a lot taller than she was now and his arms went easily round her slim body.

"Nan, you're fantastic. I do love you! ... Shall we join the others?"

The evenings were beginning to draw in and it felt as though there might be a frost. The fire was flaring high as they entered through one door and Bard Emrys entered through the other.

He was a big man, in his mid-forties, and he had collected a horrific wound across his face during the Roman attack on Ynys Mon about six years before. He came to Nanhyfer to teach Hywel how to develop his mind skills and they had become very close friends but he teased and bullied Hywel unmercifully with enthusiastic assistance from his grandmother.

"Should I bow to you, grovel or just tell you that you were a fool not to use your mind skills on your two tormentors? They were unfair to you and you were well within your rights to retaliate," he said privately into Hywel's mind as he responded to Elen's welcome.

"I thought about it long and hard. But I hated them so much that I was frightened that I wouldn't know when to stop retaliating and there was a serious danger that I'd give myself away. I'm fed up with them. Let's drop it and enjoy ourselves instead."

"Mind your manners!"

"Lord, I apologise. Please may I have your most gracious permission to enjoy myself?"

The bard grinned as they all settled down around a heavily loaded table and the conversation became general. The food was fantastic. Elen had gradually taken over the management of the household from Hywel's grandmother and she served very special dishes that she used to prepare for her family in Lydney. She mixed different sorts of meats in unfamiliar ways and some of her sauces made Hywel's mouth water just thinking about them. He forgot about making conversation and concentrated entirely on his food. He did full justice to every dish and, for the first time in over three weeks, began to feel really full and even a bit bloated. As he stretched his legs under the table and eased his belt, he became aware of a serious conversation going on around him.

"I'm really worried, Owain," said his grandmother.

"Me too," agreed his father. "I reckon it should be one pig and at least two sheep."

"No," added Tegwyn. "There will have to be at least one cow too."

Hywel was utterly bewildered and sent an enquiring glance to his grandmother.

"We were just working out how much food we needed to prepare for your supper tomorrow, Hywel," she said, smiling widely. "We do not seem to have got enough ready for you today."

Hywel went scarlet in embarrassment as the laughter broke around him.

"Not to worry, Hywel," said Elen. "We are well stocked for the feast of Samhain on the last day of October so it's no problem."

"You're a horrible lot!" he protested. "I've been starving for ages and the food was some of the best that I've ever tasted. I'm sorry I forgot to talk but eating was more important."

"Of course it was, Hywel," said Elen. "Ignore them Let's go and make music."

They played and sang late into the evening until everyone was tired. Then Bard Emrys played delicate, haunting melodies that sounded like birds soaring in the summer sunshine, ships sailing gently towards the sunset and seals singing on their lonely beaches. Hywel drifted off to sleep where he sat and into a peaceful world of his own.

CHAPTER 3 – THE WARRIOR'S OATH

Bard Emrys had already left for Nanhyfer by the time Hywel got up the next morning. He had a quick breakfast and then found his father sitting on the outside bench waiting for him.

"What happened in Gloucester, Father? You said it was important."

"Yes, it is. We've lost our best contact there - Marcus, the chief of staff, has been recalled to Rome. His successor is an unpleasant individual who told me that he doesn't need me to spy for him any more. He took back the Imperial messenger's token that Marcus had given me and made it clear that I was no longer welcome in Gloucester."

"Uggh! What did Aulus say?"

"He said that he was helpless because his new aide had powerful protectors in Rome. Aulus himself is still in charge of all Roman matters in the Gloucester area and his responsibilities were recently extended to the north.

"He's a very worried man. He says that he thinks that the Emperor Nero is going mad and the politicians in Rome are joining him. Apparently, they have withdrawn the XIVth Legion, together with a force of auxiliary cavalry, from Britain to Germany because the locals are restive there. Aulus has had to lose some troops to cover the gap that they've left and he feels very weak and vulnerable.

He knows that the Celtic tribes will attack him and he's even considering withdrawing from his fort at Usk." Owain laughed grimly. "He asked me, as a personal favour, to try and find out what the Silures in Gwent are planning to do in the spring."

"So. The crunch time has come," Hywel said, thoughtfully. "It's been great fun up to now - both spying on the Romans and for them - and we haven't really done any harm to anybody. But now our friend Aulus Cornelius Calvus needs our help badly but, to give it to him, we have to betray our own people. If we stay loyal to our own people, then we betray him. What are we going to do?"

"I don't know, Hywel, and Lord Rhys and Druid Mabon are equally uncertain. One thing's for sure - we're not going to do anything in a hurry. The sailing season is just about over until the spring and that means we can't get any information to Aulus by ship in time for him to use it. I told him so before I left Gloucester.

"We could go to him by land, if we chose to, but that would be horribly dangerous as we would have to cross Silure territory and they are on a war footing. They would kill us as spies if they caught us. However, they won't make a major attack against the Romans before the end of February so we've got time to make up our minds."

"What are we going to do about the aide's statement that we are not welcome in Gloucester any more?"

"Ignore it. The man is a political appointment and he may well have moved on by the time we go back. If he hasn't, then Aulus will stop him doing us any real harm. ... Have you still got your own messenger's token?" Hywel nodded. "Well, we'll use that if we have to. ... Don't look so miserable, boy! Today's your big day! Forget Aulus and his problems. Go and sort out your horse - he's a much more urgent problem. You need to have some control over him before we go to the llys this afternoon." Hywel grinned and nodded agreement.

It was not so easy to forget though, he thought as he collected two apples and went round to the stables. Aulus was his friend. He had spent several holidays with him and his family. He liked and trusted him. He could not just abandon him. Aulus would never abandon him. Hywel sighed. Why was life so difficult?

Mellt was in the paddock with a group of horses and Iolo was busy in the stables. He smiled happily as Hywel went in.

"Hello, sir. I'm nearly finished here. I'll be with you in a moment."

Hywel was fascinated - Iolo had not stammered at all! He swirled the last of his water over the cobbled floor, put down his bucket and came to the door.

"I've already exercised Mellt, sir. We went down to the beach and splashed in the water. He enjoys that a lot."

"Thank you, Iolo. Will you do me a favour?"

"Of course, sir."

"Stop calling me 'sir'! My name is Hywel."

"But, I can't! You're a warrior and your father is a lord. I can't call you 'Hywel'!"

"It doesn't matter what my father is. My name is still Hywel. Will you try?" he nodded, glum and red-faced. "Have an apple and come with me to talk to Mellt."

Mellt came across the field to meet them. He saw the apple in Hywel's hand and nuzzled him. Hywel had decided on an all out attack, both with his voice and his mind. His mind skills worked even better on animals than on people - except on cats; he couldn't touch them.

"Stand still, Mellt, you great hunk of dog meat. Yes, dog meat. That's what you'll be if you don't accept that I'm your master!"

The horse took a startled step backwards, looking at Hywel in astonishment.

"I said stand still! I promise that I will keep you well, feed you properly and take you to see interesting things but, in return, you must do what I say. Do you agree?"

Mellt stood rigid and glared with reddening eyes.

"Do you want Iolo to stay?" continued Hywel. "If you do, then behave yourself." Iolo turned to Hywel with a cry of distress but he ignored him, holding Mellt with his eyes. "Well, Mellt - am I your master?"

The red glare died out of the horse's eyes; he dipped his head, stepped forward and rubbed his forehead against Hywel's tunic.

"Good boy," said Hywel quietly. He fondled and patted him then gave him the apple that he demolished with two loud crunches.

"Right. Let's get organised. I'd like a ride this morning before I have to get changed to go to the llys. Iolo - would you get Mellt's saddle and bridle, please?"

Hywel was very soon mounted and cantering towards the ford that gives access to the land on the north side of the Afon Nyfer. This is very good riding country. The land climbs quite steeply up to a plateau that is covered in short, springy grass but, at the western end, it continues to climb to the peak of Foel Fach.

Mellt made light of the slope and stretched out into a gallop as they got to the plateau. They were very soon on top of the peak and Hywel's spirits soared. There was a brisk breeze that smelt fresh and salty and he could feel his chest expanding to enjoy it. The view was fantastic with the sea fading to a soft purple horizon. On the coast, Trefdraeth basked at the foot of Mynydd Carningli that towered over it protectively.

Hywel had found the last three weeks, when he had been hemmed in by trees, almost suffocating. This seemed to free his spirit and he felt light and bubbly. Mellt seemed to feel the same way and they cantered comfortably along the cliffs towards the north for the best part of an hour before turning back for home.

An anxious Iolo came out to meet them but his face spread into a broad grin as Hywel slid to the ground.

"Yes, Iolo, it's fine and we are close to being friends. I'll need him again late this afternoon to go to Nanhyfer and I'll probably spend the night at the llys. Would you look after him for me in the meantime, please?"

"Of course, sir."

Hywel felt extremely smart as he rode to the llys with his father and his uncle Tegwyn. He was wearing a new tunic, trews and a smart leather belt with a copper buckle. His cloak was also new and his grandmother had given him a large ornate pin to secure it with. But the best bit of all was the new gold torc that he wore around his neck.

The hall of the llys was full of noise and people when they arrived and Hywel was led away to wait at one side with his colleagues. A warrior briefed them:

"When everything is ready, a horn blows and Lord Rhys comes in and stands near Lord Pryderi over there, by the end wall. You stand in a line across the hall facing him in the order that you got home from your last test - that means that you are at the far end, Hywel." He nodded and the warrior continued to describe the ceremony.

"The only tricky bit is after Lord Rhys has given you your sword when you have to get up off your knees without falling over. Come through here, out of sight of everyone, and try it with my sword."

He was right; it was dead tricky! After they had all practised it, he led them back into the hall and positioned them in their line.

The horn blast nearly deafened Hywel. It was the big battle horn - not designed for use indoors! Lord Rhys came in and stood facing them and the warriors packed the hall behind them. Rhys was a tall, slim, imposing man in his late forties. His closely trimmed black hair was going grey at his temples now but he still moved with the grace of an athlete. Unusually for his tribe he was clean-shaven and he dressed very plainly.

He raised his hand and the warriors started a slow chant. Hywel swallowed hard and joined in, his voice lost in the low growl of the adults.

"I swear that I will live with honour. … I swear that I will defend the weak. … I swear that I will give my life to protect anyone who has sworn this oath." Then, after a long pause, "WARRIOR!"

The hair on the back of Hywel's neck prickled and he shivered. There was no doubt at all that every man present was speaking from a deep, almost fanatical, conviction.

Lord Pryderi gestured to Hywel. He stepped forward, bowed and fell to his knees in front of Lord Rhys who stretched out both hands. Hywel raised his hands and placed them between his lord's before looking up into his face.

He was smiling slightly as Hywel started to speak in a whisper that gradually got louder:

"Lord, I swear allegiance to you. I swear to obey your orders. I swear to defend you unto my own death."

Rhys was looking deep into his eyes, almost into his soul, as he spoke and Hywel could not look away. His smile had vanished and Hywel felt as though he was being weighed against a measure that he could not understand.

"I accept your allegiance, Hywel ap Owain ap Meredith," said Lord Rhys.

He released Hywel's hands and took a sword from Lord Pryderi.

"I give you your sword. Use it with honour. ... Stand up, warrior of Cemais! "

Hywel managed it without dropping his sword or stumbling. Rhys nodded so Hywel bowed and returned to his place in the line.

He felt weird, almost detached from himself as he watched his colleagues swear. He knew Lord Rhys well but this was not the pleasant, kindly man who had treated him like a grandson. It was a remote, austere commander with whom he now had an unbreakable bond: a bond that went beyond liking and respect. Truly, Hywel would die for him.

The last of his colleagues had just stepped back into the line when the noise started. First the stamping - a deep drumming noise.

Then the warriors started their battle cry as a growl deep in their throats, gradually raising it to a scream and ending with a defiant shout:

"Keeeeeeeeee - MAIS!"

They did again and again until Hywel's head spun. It was barbaric, terrifying, exhilarating and it raised emotions that he did not recognise. He was quivering like a hunting hound held on a tight leash and his eyes were watering.

Then Lord Rhys raised his hand. The noise stopped like a thunderclap. ...He spoke:

"I welcome these eight young warriors into the full community of our tribe. I am sure that they will bring nothing but honour to its name." He paused.

"WELCOME!" barked the warriors.

"I invite their fathers to dine with me privately tonight," continued Rhys. "Lord Pryderi will host the warrior's feast. Please do not wreck my hall during your celebrations."

He grinned at the roar of laughter that greeted his words and then started to move around the hall, talking to people as he went.

Duach, Gwyn and Hywel slipped out of the hall and found themselves a quiet corner where they sat in silence for a while. Duach was the first to speak:

"I didn't realise it was going to be like that!"

"Me neither," replied Gwyn. "I'm all mixed up. I don't know whether I want to laugh or cry. I do know one thing though. ... I'm glad it's over. I'd prefer any torture to going through that again!"

Hywel did not want to talk so he drew his sword out of its scabbard and took a couple of practice swings. It was beautifully balanced and fitted his hand perfectly. The three swords were very similar but the scabbards and hilts were decorated with their personal totem symbols - Hywel's is a seal, Duach's is a boar and Gwyn's is a stag.

They put the swords on and adjusted the shoulder belts to fit. Then they practised making fierce, warrior-type faces at each other. They collapsed into giggles when the master-at-arms unexpectedly came round the corner of the building and caught them at it.

"Well, well, boys. You've terrified me - your growls were particularly impressive, Hywel." They grinned at him happily. "I just came to tell you, all three, that I'm very proud of you. You really did me credit. Will you be joining the warrior practice sessions in the spring - just to keep current?"

"Yes, sir." replied Gwyn immediately. "And I'd also like to learn about forts, how to construct and destroy them, if you have time to teach me."

"Me too, sir," said Duach, "when I'm at home. But I'd like to know about fighting from chariots, not forts. Forts are boring."

"You can't break into a fort with a chariot!" said Gwyn scornfully. "You need your sword and spear and you need to be able to scale defended walls. Chariots are only good to carry you to a battle - not to fight it!"

"The Iceani did a pretty good job with chariots when they destroyed that Roman legion," said Duach hotly. "And … "

Hywel broke in.

"Shut up, the pair of you! Don't get into a fight now - especially with real swords in your hands. Calm down! Let's go and find the feast."

The master-at-arms smiled approvingly.

"Hywel's right. Watch your tempers all the time now. Keep your anger for an enemy. ... You'll need to leave your swords in the guardroom before you go into the feast as no weapons are allowed in the hall, except for ceremonial purposes. "

The hall was now full of trestle tables, long benches and about sixty warriors from all over the cantref. Some groups of friends were already seated and had started to drink. Others were standing around, talking and laughing in loose groups, and the three boys were drawn into different groups.

Hywel's included Lord Pryderi and a huge, laughing man with long, beautifully groomed moustaches who was swapping insults with Tegwyn. His torc was nearly as thick as Owain's and both his arms were covered in gold arm rings. Hywel stood quietly watching them until Tegwyn left and Lord Pryderi noticed him.

"Ah! Hywel," said Pryderi, "I don't think that you've met Camlach ap Clud who is the champion warrior of the cantref. His lands lie down to the southeast and he rarely comes to Nanhyfer. He wanted to meet you tonight."

"How do you do, sir?" Hywel said politely, looking up at him in awe.

In battle, the champions fight each other first with the opposing armies looking on. Sometimes they fight naked, as they believe that this gives them extra strength and sometimes a successful champion will fight a succession of warriors from the other side until no more challengers can be found. When this happens, that army normally gives up and goes home without fighting because the gods are obviously not supporting them. Camlach had a fantastic reputation and no one had been prepared to challenge him for years.

"So you're young Hywel ap Owain are you?" he replied. "Your uncle Tegwyn is an old sparring partner of mine. Has he told you how I stole the junior championship off him by grabbing the stake while he distracted the sentry?" Camlach laughed - a throaty rumble from deep down inside him. Hywel nodded. "He was furious! We fought then and we fought again when the last champion died in a hunting accident. That time it was serious because we were fighting for the real championship. We were very evenly matched and I was extremely lucky to win."

"He did not tell me that part, sir. I had no idea that he was that good!"

Camlach grinned.

"You've a lot to live up to, boy! It's time we took our seats. Come on."

He led him to a seat at the centre of the top table and Lord Pryderi followed them.

Hywel pulled back.

"I can't sit here, sir! My place is down with the small fry!"

"No it isn't. We champions must stick together. Sit down!"

Hywel sat between him and Lord Pryderi, feeling terribly uncomfortable but, before he could protest any further, the horn sounded again and the hall fell silent.

Lord Pryderi stood up and announced in a loud voice:

"The Champion's Portion!"

Traditionally, the champion is given the biggest and best portion of food, both on the battlefield and at ceremonial feasts. Two young pages entered the hall carrying a whole side of roast pork between them on a large silver dish. They put it down on the table in front of Camlach, bowed and left. He stood and looked around the hall before speaking in a deep, carrying voice:

"Fellow warriors. Tonight I share my portion with the junior champion of the cantref. Drink to Hywel ap Owain ap Meredith!"

"HYWEL!" the warriors roared back and then started to cheer.

Hywel was flabbergasted and wanted the floor to open under him. He had not realised that being the junior champion brought this sort of attention and he did not want it either! He started to get to his feet, with the firm intention of escaping through the nearest door, but Camlach's hand pressed down on his shoulder so that he could not move and had to sit there and take it.

Camlach and Pryderi were very kind to Hywel for the rest of the feast and, when he explained that he hated getting drunk, Pryderi sent a page to fetch him water in the same sort of flagon that they were using for wine so that nobody else would know.

Bard Emrys played his harp for a while and the warrior's singing nearly raised the rafters. Then the feast got very noisy as people moved around to talk to different friends and the serious drinking started.

Hywel slipped out of the hall apparently to answer a call of nature and then sat on the rampart to talk to the stars. The two oaths he had sworn so recently made his problems with his Roman friend even worse. All Celtic warriors swore similar oaths. How could he betray them to Aulus? But, wait a minute! ... Celtic warriors often fought and killed each other. ... How did that fit with their oaths?

"Thinking of oaths, Hywel?" asked Bard Emrys in a low voice as he sat down beside him.

"I thought I'd got my mind block up against you," said Hywel softly.

"You have. It was a logical deduction on my part, no mind skills needed."

"Well, you're right. How can warriors who have made that oath ever fight and kill each other?"

"I don't know. I'm only a bard and I have different loyalties. But I believe that your oath to Lord Rhys over-rides your oath to unknown warriors."

"That seems reasonable ... but I need to think about it some more." They sat in companionable silence for a while until Hywel remembered something else that had been bothering him.

"Emrys?" The bard grunted. "Emrys, before you came here, Druid Mabon banished a boy who tried to kill me. But I saw him back here the other day. Why has Mabon changed his mind?"

"Pebyn you mean?"

"Yes."

"Two reasons. Firstly, Pebyn's father died recently and Pebyn is his heir. Secondly, Mabon wasn't able to punish him properly for his attack on you four years ago because he was a minor at law. Pebyn is now fourteen and legally an adult, even if he is too incompetent to be a warrior. But if he does anything stupid again, then Mabon will throw the full weight of the law at him. I wouldn't worry too much. He is only here for a couple of days to visit his mother. Then he will be going back to the Irish chief who is visiting the king of Dyfed at the moment. For some strange reason he seems to have semi-adopted Pebyn."

"I hope you are right. I can't stand Pebyn - he makes my flesh creep - and I trust him as far as I can throw my horse. The sooner he goes away again the better. That Irishman must be crazy!"

Hywel left the hall before any of the other revellers woke the next morning and went to see the master-at-arms.

"Sir, yesterday you offered us advanced warrior training." He nodded encouragingly. "Well, I need training but not as a warrior."

"What sort, then?"

"You know that I sail with my father to strange places? We go there as traders and traders don't carry weapons so we can't either."

"You mean that you go there as spies? Yes, I know that. It's been a fairly open secret since you brought back that escaped prisoner-of-war about four years ago."

"Well, is there anyone who can teach me to fight without weapons? I can use my fists and I can wrestle a bit but I need more than that. I need to be able to defend myself against people like robbers who would use clubs or knives."

"I understand. Unfortunately, my specialist, Iorwerth ap Rhys, is away at the moment but I'll fix it with him when he gets back."

The master-at-arms was looking past Hywel as he spoke. He started to grin and then, if such a term can be attached to such an important man, he started to giggle.

"Oh …! Look, Hywel! Have you ever seen anything like it?"

A very sick looking Gwyn was moving slowly past them on his horse. He wasn't exactly riding it. He sat slumped in his saddle with the reins slack in his hands and he winced every time that the horse took a step. Fortunately, the horse seemed to know where it was going because Gwyn had his eyes shut most of the time. Every couple of paces he let out a low moan.

"He obviously enjoyed last night's feast too well. You'd better go and look after him, Hywel. He'll never get home without help."

"Serves him right," laughed Hywel. "But I'll rescue him. Thanks for your help, sir. I appreciate it."

Gwyn managed to make it as far as Hywel's house without collapsing. Hywel's grandmother, Rhiannon, smiled and shook her head in exasperation when she saw him. Then she went into the house and came back with a mug of herb-smelling liquid in her hand.

"Drink that, boy! It will make you feel better, though I don't know why I should save you from your own follies. ... Go on, drink it." Gwyn groaned and obeyed. "Now sit quiet for a bit until your head feels better."

"I want to die," croaked Gwyn miserably. "The only good thing is that Duach is worse than I am. Uggghh!!! Never again! I want to die."

They laughed at him and he groaned again. He gradually began to feel better and Rhiannon bullied him into eating a meal of bread, milk and honey, after which he began to recover properly.

"I will never do that again," he said as he went to mount his horse. "I didn't really enjoy it at the time but I didn't want to say no when they kept filling my mug - I thought it was the grown up thing to do. Grown up or not, it was stupid - never again. ... Goodbye, Hywel, and thanks."

A couple of mornings later Hywel went round to the stables early. The air had a hint of frost but the sky was a clear powder blue without a cloud in sight and the gorse and heather on the hilltops shone in the sunlight.

He set off for Duach's house feeling exhilarated and at one with the world. Mellt seemed to share his feelings and they moved in complete harmony of both minds and bodies.

Mellt was interested in everything that they saw as the route was new to him and Hywel was quite certain that he would have no difficulty in finding his own way back without any guidance.

Duach came out to greet them and let out a low whistle of approval when he saw Mellt; they had not met before.

"Isn't he a beauty? ... My father gave me one too - a chestnut that could be this one's brother. His name is Saeth - which means arrow. Come and see."

He led them round to the stable where an intelligent chestnut head with a white blaze whickered a welcome over a half door. Mellt rubbed noses while the boys admired both of them.

"Where shall we go?" asked Duach, automatically assuming that they were going to spend the day on horseback.

"Let's get up onto the moors where we'll have room to move - perhaps up towards Brynberian?"

"Fine. I'll just go and grab some food to take with us. I won't be a minute."

They were soon climbing the steep slope to the south of Duach's house. Both horses were pressing hard to take the lead but, as they were very evenly matched, they went up the steep hill shoulder to shoulder. Once they got up onto the plateau the boys let the horses gallop until they slowed down at their own accord and then they had a very comfortable ride at an easy pace for the rest of the morning.

They carefully skirted the enormous cairn at Pentre Ifan that loomed on a shoulder of the hill to their right - Hywel was not sure which was more scary, the cairn or the four huge outcrops of rock on the summit which guard it. The druids say that these cairns are the graves of the Old Ones who lived in the land in the time before time, and there are a lot of them, but this one is by far the biggest and it is thought to be the grave of giants. No sensible person ever went anywhere near it, not even the druids. Hywel's own Cairn Briw on the top of Mynydd Carningli was about a quarter of the size and a lot more friendly.

They had a long break for lunch at Brynberian which is a pleasant little village on the edge of the tree line and, almost, on the edge of civilisation. It lies on flat marshy land that collects all the water that streams off the slopes of Mynydd Preseli in vast quantities for most of the year. The mountains themselves form a high, bare arc louring over the village and, although there are forts and settlements near the trackway that runs along the line of the summits, they can't be seen from below.

It would be all too easy to imagine bad-tempered monsters looking down and watching your every move. Hywel thought to himself. Monsters did exist here not too long ago and one is buried under the cairn at Bedd yr Afanc that was about a kilometre south of where they were sitting.

Duach's voice broke into Hywel's depressing thoughts.

"What are we going to do now that we've got our swords and the feast is over?"

"Swear not to get drunk again?" asked Hywel

Duach threw a half-hearted punch at him.

"I'm so ashamed of myself, Hywel. I was a complete fool. Never again. What happened to you?"

"Oh, I saved myself because I told Lord Pryderi that I didn't want to get drunk. To my surprise, he accepted it without turning a hair and got me water to drink instead. No problem."

"I wish I'd thought of that but I doubt that my neighbours would have been so co-operative. Well, what are we going to do?"

"I hadn't really thought about it. ... As soon as our sailing master, Gruffydd, thinks that the time is right, we are due to start overhauling our three ships and getting them ready for the winter. Everyone he can lay his hands on takes part in the worst bit - scraping weed and barnacles off the hulls - it has to be done fast as the ships are hauled onto their sides so that we can get in between the twin keels at low tide and a change in the weather could cause a disaster. I hate it because my father insists that the family works in the most dangerous spot, right at the bottom of the keels. I'm always convinced that the ship is going to fall on top of me, even though I know that Gruffydd would never let it happen. ... I would be exceedingly grateful if you could think of something that would get me out of it!"

"I'll work on it - but don't hold your breath. It's very difficult to change your father's mind once he's decided on something."

They got back to Duach's house just as his own father was riding in from Nanhyfer. He greeted them pleasantly and made a fuss of Mellt. Grooms took the three horses away and the boys followed him into the house.

"Well, Duach," he said, as soon as he was seated comfortably. "We are off again the day after tomorrow."

Duach's father, Bedwyr, is Lord Rhys' chief advisor and ambassador. He deals with most matters outside the cantref and Duach, as his apprentice, has travelled all over Wales in his company.

"Great! Where are we going?"

"Not far," said Bedwyr with a yawn. "Just to the llys of Deugleddyf at Hwlffordd. Apparently, the king of Dyfed is staying there at the moment and he wants to see all his chiefs in four days time. Lord Rhys doesn't want to go but he doesn't have any choice and he won't move without us."

"Why a meeting, Father? The king doesn't normally want his chiefs; their representatives are usually good enough."

"His nephew, Anwyl, who brought the message, says that the tribes of east Wales, led by the Silures think that the Romans are weak at the moment and they are planning to attack them in the spring. They want all the other tribes to join in and the king is inclined to agree. As you know, nearly all of the warriors in the kingdom owe allegiance to their chiefs and not directly to the king himself. Therefore, if the king wants troops, he has to get agreement from the chiefs. The Silures are in a hurry and want an answer now - hence the meeting. We go in state and take ten armed warriors with us."

"That should be fun. We normally only take five."

"We'll have Lord Rhys himself with us. I'd prefer to take half the cantref to protect him against the king - you know how they hate each other. But Rhys will only accept ten and I had to fight to get him to accept that many."

"Sir?" said a cautious voice.

"Yes, Hywel?"

"Sir, could I possibly come with you? I've never seen the king and … "

He trailed to a stop as he saw the expression on Bedwyr's face.

"Sorry, Hywel. You've tried all the arguments before but the answer is still no."

"But I'm a man now, sir! And a warrior! Even the Junior Champion! Doesn't that make a difference? Please?"

Bedwyr grinned and shook his head.

"No way, Hywel. Not until Druid Mabon gives his permission. When he agrees I'll be delighted to take you, but not until then."

Hywel could not understand it. High Druid Mabon had made this decree about three years ago - he was to be kept away from court - but Mabon would not tell him why and nobody would disobey the druid.

Hywel nursed his disappointment for a while but soon left and went to Nanhyfer. He would have it out with Druid Mabon. He must have a reason.

Hywel tied Mellt to the high fence that surrounded the druid's compound and rang the big bell that hangs outside the gate. A servant appeared and greeted him warmly.

"I'd like to see Druid Mabon please. Right now, if it's possible."

"I'm sorry, sir, but Druid Mabon isn't here."

Hywel cursed.

"When will he be back?"

"Sometime after Samhain if he's lucky. He's gone off to prepare himself to cross into the Otherworld. He does it every year. So far, he's always got back safely, although he looks like a skeleton when he returns. One year he'll make a mistake and we'll never see him again."

Hywel cursed again and set out for home. His anger grew as he rode back and he was furious as he stomped into his house. He would have it out with his father! It wasn't fair! He should go and see the king! Was there something wrong with him that he had to be hidden away? He was good enough to make friends with Roman generals, why could he not go and see his own king?

Owain listened to the words that poured out of him but he made Hywel even more furious when he repeated Bedwyr's words exactly with precisely the same expression on his face. Hywel was just about to storm out when he stopped him.

"You and I need to talk, Hywel. Why have you suddenly become so arrogant?"

"Arrogant, Father?"

"Yes. You wouldn't normally dream of storming off to confront Druid Mabon nor have you ever used that tone of voice to me before."

"I'm sorry. I didn't realise that I had."

Hywel looked down and examined his fingers for a long moment then looked at him with a wry grin.

"Well, ever since I can remember, I've always been worried that I wouldn't measure up to what other people expected of me - you in particular, but also my grandmother, Druid Mabon and Lord Rhys. Then during the warrior test I realised that I had survived more trials than most people, not only survived, but also coped better than most." He paused.

"True. And?"

"I decided that I was at least as good as everyone else and that I didn't care any more about what other people thought. I would make my own judgements and live with the consequences."

His father looked at him thoughtfully.

"In many ways you are right, Hywel. But you have taken your logic a couple of steps too far. As a person, you are as good as anyone else in the land, you always have been. But as a member of our tribe, you are of little importance. You are one of the youngest, untried warriors - would you back your judgement as a warrior against Camlach, the champion?" Hywel shook his head. "You are a junior seaman on one of my ships - would you back your judgement as a seaman against Gruffydd, our sailing master? He hammered on until Hywel wanted the floor to open up and swallow him. Everything he said was true but it still hurt.

"I will not accept that sort of behaviour from you again," Owain concluded in a hard voice. "You will behave with the courtesy that befits your station. Do you understand?"

Hywel nodded slowly.

"Look at me and reply properly!"

"Yes, Father. In future, I will behave with the courtesy that befits my station."

CHAPTER 4 – THE SHIELD BEARER

Hywel sat uneasily in the llys hall the next morning waiting for Lord Rhys to have time to see him. He had summoned him last night but the messenger had no idea what it was about. Hywel was still smarting from his father's comments and he wondered if Lord Rhys was about to deliver some more. If he did, Hywel thought, he would seriously consider going to live with his friend Aulus in Gloucester and he might even apply to become a Roman citizen. At least Aulus appreciated him!

A page appeared and took him to Lord Rhys.

"Come in and sit down, Hywel," he said as Hywel entered and bowed to him. "We need to talk. ... Do you remember that, when you came back from your first voyage, I told you that you were special and that I intended to make you a councillor when you were ready?"

"Yes, lord, ... but I didn't think you meant it. I thought that you said it to cheer me up because I was miserable."

"No, Hywel. I meant it. As of today you are a councillor but it must stay a secret between our normal group - Druid Mabon, Bedwyr, Duach, your father and your grandmother. Understand?"

"Yes, lord," he gulped and wondered what on earth was going to happen to him next. First a kick in the teeth from his father and now a compliment from Lord Rhys! He did not think that there could be any more surprises left - but he was wrong!

"It is a bit sooner than I intended," said Lord Rhys, "but I need you fully in my confidence before we go to see the king." Hywel stared at him in amazement. "I can not take Druid Mabon with me so I need you to do two things for me there. Firstly, to monitor the thoughts of the king and his councillors and to let me know the gist of them. Secondly, to monitor the minds of the other nobles who are at court. All right so far?"

"Yes, lord," whispered Hywel.

"I have deliberately kept you away from court for the past three years in the hope that people will think that you are unimportant and, as a result, will ignore you. In a way, you have helped my plan by doing so well in the warrior tests - nobody will think that it is strange that I should take the junior champion as my shield-bearer. Shield-bearers are purely decorative and stand behind their chiefs during important conferences - you will be perfectly positioned to see and hear everything that goes on. But look bored and stupid so that nobody can guess what you are really doing."

"Looking stupid should be no problem, lord," said Hywel who had never felt more stupid in his life.

"I want you to use your judgement about what you feed into my mind during the meetings - I do not need everything, just the important parts. We can catch up later on the other thoughts that you collect. Wandering around the minds of the lesser nobles could be equally important and we will arrange a time each day for you to brief me. All right?"

"Yes, lord. Monitoring minds should be easy enough but I'm scared about using my own judgement. I don't think that I know enough to decide what is, or is not, important to you."

"I understand, but just do your best. You will soon see what is bluster and nonsense. Some of the chiefs are narrow minded and stupid - you need not waste any time on them. Others are very wily and need to be watched carefully." He then went on to describe the various people that they would meet and how he classified them until Hywel had a reasonable idea of their relative importance.

"I am worried, Hywel," he concluded. "Nothing fits properly. The king is up to something and I cannot work out what it is. I believe that the messenger from the Silures is just an excuse. I need you to find out the real reason for the meeting, if you can."

"I'll do my very best, lord, but wouldn't Druid Mabon be of more use to you?"

"No, Hywel," he grinned. "Mabon is better at home, for a variety of reasons. Go and talk it over with your grandmother. She can explain it better than I can. ... We leave at dawn tomorrow. Come and stay here tonight and bring a groom with you. All right?"

"Yes, lord. Thank you." He bowed and took his leave.

He rode back home as fast as he could and, as Mellt caught his urgency, that was very fast indeed. They were still moving at a dangerous speed as they clattered into the stables. A very surprised Iolo came out to greet them and he looked even more surprised when Hywel tied Mellt to a post.

"Iolo," he said. "Leave Mellt for a moment. We need to talk. I'm going with Lord Rhys tomorrow to see the king. He says that I can take a groom with me. Would you like to come?"

"M... m.... me?" he stammered. "But I won't know what to do! I've never even seen a king!"

"That's not important; you'll be with me. Would you like to come?"

He nodded, wide-eyed.

"Yes, please, sir, if you think that I'll be able to manage."

"Of course you will. Now, you're going to need clothes - a decent tunic and a cloak - have you got any?"

Iolo looked at Hywel in dismay.

"No, sir. I've only got this one tunic and I use an old horse blanket as a cloak when it's really cold."

"Come on, then. Let's go and see my stepmother. She'll find some clothes that I've outgrown that should fit you reasonably well. Then come back here, sort out Mellt and chose a sturdy pony for yourself. I'll borrow two saddlebags from my father and you can use one of them for your own things. We go to the llys at Nanhyfer for supper and spend the night there before leaving at dawn tomorrow. All right?" Iolo gulped and nodded, then followed Hywel into the house. Hywel left him with Elen and went to find his grandmother.

She listened carefully to all that he had to tell her, smiling at him fondly until he concluded with: "But I still don't really know why he wants to take me with him instead of Druid Mabon. He said that you would explain it to me, Nan. Do you know why?"

"There are several reasons, Hywel. Firstly, Lord Rhys genuinely wants you as his councillor, his wife told me so. Secondly, Mabon has started to withdraw into himself as he always does at this time of the year. As you know, during Samhain, the division between this world and the Otherworld dissolves and people can pass freely between the two existences. Sometimes they get stuck on the wrong side when Samhain finishes and then they are trapped on one side or the other for whole of the following year. Otherworld refugees become the evil spirits that plague us sometimes. Mabon wanders extensively in the Otherworld but he prepares himself carefully so that he can meet the spirits he wants to talk to and, more importantly, so that he can find his way back to this world. He tends to go off into a trance and he is completely lost to us until he decides to return. But thirdly, and most importantly, Mabon insulted the king during his election by calling him a soft-minded fool. Although Mabon was right, the king has never forgiven him and he won't have him anywhere near him!"

"Election, Nan? I thought that kings took over from their fathers. I didn't realise they were elected."

"Well, normally the oldest sons inherit but they do not have to. Officially, a new king or a chief can be the uncle, brother, son or nephew of the old one. This king was the oldest son but all his brothers and uncles were better men. The family could not agree who should take over so the chiefs were consulted. Lord Rhys and Mabon argued strongly against the present king - they preferred a younger brother who has since died - but the other chiefs did not agree. They decided that they did not want a strong, effective king, as he would interfere too much in their own affairs. So they chose the present one - who hates everyone who comes from Cemaes. He can not stop Rhys attending the conference, because he is too powerful, but do not expect him to make you welcome!"

"Thank you," Hywel said thoughtfully. "I understand much better now. But that means that I don't automatically take over from my father as chief of Carningli - it could be uncle Tegwyn or one of the twins. I hadn't realised that before."

"Yes. Some families fight over the succession and sometimes they kill each other off and the inheritance passes to a remote relative. The division of land is different but we'll talk about it another day. You will need to understand the family relationships between the various nobles at court if you are to do the job that Lord Rhys wants you to do – we will talk about that later too."

"And I thought that he was doing me a favour by taking me there. It promises to be an even more interesting visit than I thought it would be!" He smiled at her wryly and left her to find his father to tell him the news.

"That's great, Hywel. I'm delighted for you." He did not really look delighted; he was frowning thoughtfully. "I'm glad we had that talk yesterday. This makes what I had to say even more important. You're riding very high at the moment - junior champion, councillor, favourite of Lord Rhys - but don't forget - you're really only a temporary, very junior aide to him. When you get back, you revert to normal and you'll be scrubbing ships' bottoms with everyone else - no favours, no special treatment, just mucky, hard, physical work. Understand?"

"Yes, of course, Father," he said, in surprise.

"You threw a temper tantrum yesterday and you showed a marked lack of judgement. Control your temper while you are away. Don't get into any fights. Stay in the background and keep out of trouble. Understand?"

"Yes, Father."

"I'll check with Bedwyr when you get back. If I find that you have disobeyed me in any way, I will confine you alone on one of our empty ships for as long as I think is necessary. Understand?"

"Yes, Father." That was a horrendous threat. The empty ships are moored in the middle of the river for the winter with their masts removed. Because they are

- 57 -

empty, they bounce around in the wind like unstable cockleshells until even the most experienced sailors get very sick. It is too dangerous to have a fire on board so they are cold and very damp. Also, it is impossible to heat food on board - that is if Owain intended to produce any food! For the first time in his life Hywel felt really scared of his father.

Owain smiled at him.

"Keep out of trouble, boy, and it won't happen. ... Now, let's find some money for you to take with you."

Iolo brought the horses up to the house long before they were needed but they left anyway as Hywel wanted to get away from his father - those two interviews had really unsettled him. Hywel spent most of the ride to the llys reassuring Iolo but the boy was edgy, uncertain and stammering badly when they met the duty groom in the llys stables.

"Don't worry, sir," said the man, with a beaming smile, "I'll make sure that he's fed and watered and that he has everything ready for you in good time tomorrow. Come on, youngster. Let's fix these horses." Unfortunately, Mellt had picked up Iolo's fears and started playing up. Hywel had to speak to him very severely before he agreed to enter the stable. He left them to it and went to find his own supper.

The llys was a hive of activity long before dawn the next morning. Hywel made a quick breakfast and went around to the stables to see if Iolo had survived. He was scurrying around happily under the direction of a stocky grey haired man who greeted Hywel cheerfully.

"Good morning, sir. I'm Rhun ap Echel and I'm the horsemaster for this trip. Your boy has settled in fine and your horse is ready for you. Isn't he a beauty! He won't let me near him but Iolo can control him with a word. I've given the boy a pack horse to lead on the journey, if that's all right with you?"

"Yes, of course. How many of us will there be altogether?"

"Well, Lord Rhys and yourself, Lord Bedwyr and Duach; each of you will have a groom and both lords will have two servants as well. That's twelve, thirteen with me, not counting the ten warriors of the escort. We'll have five packhorses to carry food, drink, gifts for the king, Lord Rhys' ceremonial shield and the lords' personal gear. We pick up Lord Bedwyr's party as we go past his house."

Hywel whistled in surprise.

"So many?"

"It would have been three times as many with the old Lord. He really enjoyed travelling in state. I remember my father talking about parties of fifty, but they needed big escorts in those days, as the land was dangerous. Lord Rhys doesn't like too much show so I don't get very many opportunities to be a horsemaster. But we should be moving, sir. Will you lead your horse?"

Iolo was standing close by, holding a restless Mellt.

"I've told him how important it is that he should be good today, sir, but I'm not sure that he believed me. He's very excited and I haven't had a chance to exercise him."

"Not to worry, Iolo. I'll exercise him hard until he calms down." Hywel turned to Rhun. "How much time do I have?"

"Well, Lord Rhys' servant hasn't brought his personal gear over yet. ... Up and down the hill and across to the bridge but no more. I'll start moving the horses out as soon as you reach the bottom of the hill on the way back. All right?"

"Thanks a lot." He mounted Mellt and they were soon racing dangerously fast down the steep path, across to the bridge and back again. It worked and Mellt was blowing hard as they slithered to a halt in front of the llys. Hywel talked to Mellt seriously during the few minutes they had to wait for Lord Rhys and the horse took its position in the cavalcade quite docilely.

Bedwyr and his party were mounted and waiting on the path outside his house. Duach and Hywel fell in behind the two lords as they led the way towards Brynberian. The escort commander joined the two boys as they reached the plateau.

"I need to brief you, boys, on what I want you to do during the journey. I know you've heard it before, Duach, but it's a bit different now that we've got Hywel with us."

"No problem, sir." said Duach cheerfully.

"Well, you two are the close escort and you are responsible for protecting the two lords with your lives. You stay close to them, no matter what happens elsewhere. Right?" They nodded. "Eight of the escort are out about half a kilometre - two pairs ahead as scouts matched by two more pairs behind. I will ride just behind you with another pair so that I can co-ordinate our defence. If anything happens, the horsemaster will bunch up the servants and bring them close to us so that we have a smaller target to defend. Clear?" They nodded again. "Nothing will happen within the cantref, particularly as we have had a five-man warband patrolling the border since early yesterday, but I'm not so sure outside it and I'm not taking any chances at all. I don't want to be known as the warrior who lost his chief, so you two stay close and obey my orders implicitly. Right?"

"Yes, sir," they chorused and he dropped behind.

The party swung southwest before it reached Brynberian and the lords broke into an easy canter as they climbed up the long slope to the standing stones and the outlying farm at Tafarn-y-bwlch. The scout escorts matched their movements but the servants and the packhorses started to fall behind. Hywel could hear the escort commander cursing under his breath as his careful plan fell apart. The pace slowed as the gradient steepened towards the pass and the ground deteriorated. It was a spooky place, mostly marsh sprinkled generously with heather hags and huge grey boulders covered with scabs of yellow lichen. The sky had clouded over and the wind was damp and piercing.

Suddenly a horseman appeared well to their right on the summit of Cerrig Lladron. The escort commander's curses grew in intensity, but not in volume, until the horseman raised his spear and twisted it round in a vertical circle.

"Good," said Duach, "that's the all clear signal. I'd hate to have to fight over this ground. We should meet the rest of his warband soon." They were waiting in a sheltered hollow, just over the top of the pass. Their leader rode forward and saluted Lord Rhys.

"Everything is clear around us here, lord, and you can safely rest the horses. But there is a problem lower down. You see the clearing below the tree line slightly to our right?" Lord Rhys nodded. "Well, twenty men armed with shields, swords and spears went into it a couple of hours after dawn. They weren't a hunting party as they didn't have any dogs with them – nor did they carry bows - they were definitely a strong warband ready for a fight. You can't see any of them at the moment but none of them has come out yet. I haven't investigated as it's just over the cantref boundary and I needed your instructions first."

Lord Rhys grunted and dismounted. Hywel led his horse away and tended to both it and to Mellt because the grooms and servants were still making their way slowly up the slope. Duach dealt his own and with Bedwyr's horse and the two boys then rejoined the lords and the two warrior commanders.

"It looks very much like an ambush to me, lord, although we haven't seen any of them cross to the other side of the track as they would have done if they meant to attack," said the warband leader.

"There's enough cover down there to hide an army," said the escort commander, "and they could be anywhere. They might already have a second band on the other side of the track. I recommend that we turn back, lord."

"It is just possible that they are hostile," added Bedwyr, thoughtfully. "But I believe that it is much more likely that they are a guard of honour, possibly sent by the king. He would be extremely irritated if we rejected them by turning back."

"I am not turning back," said Lord Rhys, forcefully. "You," he said, turning to the warband commander, "send two of your men down to them to investigate. They can signal back to us - or, if they disappear, we will know that those warriors are hostile. The rest of your band can join my escort.

"You," he said, turning to the escort commander, "Take command of all our warriors.

- 62 -

"And you," he said, turning to Hywel, "Get me some food."

They were a silent group as they ate their lunch and watched the two warriors ride down the slope towards the tree line. They disappeared into it and they only caught a fleeting glimpse of them as they crossed a clearing. It seemed ages before one of them eventually re-appeared and gave the all-clear signal.

"Is that your man?" Lord Rhys demanded.

"Yes, lord, I think so," replied the warband commander, uncertainly. "It's a bit difficult to see at this distance."

Lord Rhys snorted derisively. "Bring in all our scouts and get mounted as soon as they arrive. Keep our party in a tight group and keep the escort close."

They rode warily down the slope until three strange horsemen came out of the trees and rode towards them. One of them spurred ahead of the others and saluted Lord Rhys with a flourish.

"I am Dinias ap Einon, lord, and I bring greetings from my master, Modron, lord of Daugleddyf. I am commanded by him to escort you to his llys and to ensure your safety and comfort on the journey."

"I thank you, Dinias ap Einon, for your welcome and for the message you bring. I would be honoured to accept your escort. Will you ride with me?"

"One moment, lord, while I call my troop."

Lord Rhys looked at Hywel enquiringly as Dinias rode a short distance away and signalled to his troop.

"No hostile intent, lord. He belongs to Lord Modron and is nothing to do with the king. He is quite genuine - and he's terrified of you!" Hywel said into his mind.

Lord Rhys grinned broadly as he beckoned to his own escort commander.

"Send our warband back to their proper duties. Keep the escort together but have them drop back a bit. They are crowding us," he said in a low voice. The escort commander started to argue.

"But, lord! ..."

"Do you want to change places with the warband commander or even with one of these boys?" Rhys asked icily.

"No, lord." The escort commander saluted smartly and clattered away to do as he was bid.

Ten of Dinias' warriors formed up ahead of the party and the other ten took up their position behind. Bedwyr dropped back as Dinias joined Lord Rhys and the party gradually relaxed as it moved down onto lower ground and wound its way through rich farmland.

The warriors soon started to sing so the rest of the journey passed quickly and the llys came in sight in the late afternoon. It sat on top of a large, steep-sided rocky hill jutting out towards a broad river. They approached it along a plateau from the west where the land shrank to a narrow neck and then opened out again into a huge flat field that contained the hall, warrior barracks and other administrative buildings, houses, stables and grazing areas. The neck of land was cut by two deep, man-made ditches about forty metres apart and both of them were crossed by a wooden bridge. Both ditches were backed by thick wooden walls built from big trees sunk vertically in the ground and linked by trees set horizontally behind. The gates were offset so the path zigzagged between them. These were formidable defences indeed but today the gates were standing hospitably open and the defenders were lined up ceremonially to welcome Lord Rhys.

CHAPTER 5 – DAUGLEDDYF

Lord Modron was standing outside his hall with a group of richly dressed nobles waiting to welcome the Cemais party.

"Is the king with them?" Hywel whispered to Duach as they rode across the grass.

"No. Three of them are chiefs from the southern cantrefs and one is the king's nephew, Anwyl. The others must be locals."

They dismounted and grooms came forward to take the horses away. Modron greeted Rhys warmly and started introducing him to his companions. Modron was a youngish man, about the same age as Owain, of medium height, very athletic, and a bundle of energy. Hywel did not really need to check his mind to classify him as a friend; he obviously liked and respected Rhys and there was no deceit at all in his frank, open, cheerful face. He checked anyway, and was surprised to find, besides what he had expected, a vague shadow of something that he couldn't classify - unease, perhaps? Hywel did not have time to dig any deeper as Modron led the party through the big double doors into the hall.

The king was waiting on a dais at the end of the hall and Hywel studied him with interest. He was a tall, weedy man with an arrogant, sneering expression on his face. His black hair was thinning fast but his long moustaches drooped down nearly onto his tunic. He was covered in gold ornaments and precious jewels that he fingered constantly as though to re-assure himself of his wealth and power. He made an interesting contrast to Lord Rhys who was dressed simply but radiated a natural authority that needed no jewelled reinforcement to mark him out as a leader.

Hywel got into the king's mind as Rhys approached him, stopped and bowed formally. The king nodded curtly and, without saying a word, turned away to talk to a big, powerful, redheaded noble standing beside him. The king's mind was a seething, jumbled mass of hatred and envy and it was almost impossible to sort out individual thoughts. Hywel concluded that the king did not like Rhys very much and intended to humble him. How he proposed to do it was not clear but, apparently, the redhead was critical to his plans.

Modron was appalled by the king's rudeness and he moved very quickly to join Rhys who was standing alone in the middle of the hall completely relaxed with a half smile on his face. The smile broadened as he saw Modron's concern.

"Don't worry, Modron. His family never had any manners," said Rhys in a low but penetrating voice that was heard clearly by everyone in the hall. Everyone stopped breathing and you could have heard a feather fall. The silence seemed to last for an age. Then the redheaded noble laughed and guided the king out of the hall through a door at the rear.

Hywel gulped and started breathing again and Duach gave a long, silent whistle as they exchanged amazed glances. Lord Modron led Rhys to his steward who collected the rest of the party with a look and took them across to the four-roomed rectangular wooden house that had been allocated to Rhys. Its owner was waiting in the comfortable hall.

"Lord Rhys, it is a great honour to lend you my house and I hope that you will be comfortable. I've left you my cook and the kitchen staff but the rest of us are staying with relatives in the town. Your own servants have already settled in and I will leave you now." He bowed and scuttled out so fast that Rhys didn't have a chance to thank him or even to find out his name!

Rhys smiled as he sank into a comfortable chair, accepted a mug of ale from his steward and drained it in one long draught.

"Thanks, Aled. I needed that. I hope I didn't frighten that poor man too much. How are things?"

"No, lord. You didn't frighten him at all. Just the idea of having you here blew his mind! But the house is comfortable. There are two big rooms with a bed and a pallet in each - we can move the pallets out into the hall for the two young masters if you wish. I've put bowls of hot water in both rooms for you to wash and you are expected in the hall for a feast at dusk. ... Oh, one thing more. The commander of the escort is about to set a sentry outside the front door."

"What a idiot!" exploded Rhys. "Get him for me as soon as you can. Leave the pallets where they - unless the boys snore. Do you?" They grinned and shook their heads. Aled ran off on his errand and they helped themselves to the ale that he had left on the table. Hywel and Duach kept silent and faded into the background as far as they could - this was no time to cross Lord Rhys!

"You sent for me, lord?" said the escort commander after he had entered and saluted formally.

"Yes. You are a fool! Mounting a sentry of our own within this llys is an insult to Lord Modron and so is carrying weapons. You should know better. Take that sentry away and keep him away. Stay out of my sight yourself until I send for you. Is that clear?"

The warrior flushed scarlet.

"Yes, lord," he replied, bowed and left hastily.

"Right, boys. You will eat in the hall tonight amongst the small fry. I would like you to go and check that the grooms and horses survived the journey but I will not need you for anything else until dawn tomorrow. You may go." They bowed and left.

"What a welcome!" said Duach in disbelief. "I've never seen anything like it."

Hywel shook his head in amazement.

"My grandmother said that they hated each other but that was something else! One word from either of them and our weapons would have been out!"

"Yes. And I'm not sure that we would have won. We need to watch our step until we know who are our friends."

"And our enemies! ... Ouch! I hurt from that new saddle! Let's go and find the horsemaster."

He was sitting on a bale of hay, with a chunk of bread in one hand and a mug of ale in the other, directing the activities of his grooms. He greeted them cheerfully and made room for them on his bale.

"How were your new saddles?" he asked innocently.

"Full of rocks," Hywel replied. "You haven't brought any liniment with you, have you?"

He guffawed.

"Yes, horse liniment." He laughed again as the boys groaned. "It works fine on people too - stings a bit though. Do you want some?"

"Yes, please."

He went and fetched a large jar of strong smelling liquid and a bucket of water. "Wash yourselves first and then rub this in hard. Don't frighten the horses with your squeals. Do you want Iolo to attend to the bits you can't reach?"

"No way, thanks! We'll sort out each other," Hywel replied indignantly.

"But before we do," said Duach, "Lord Rhys wants to know how everybody is and if the horses are all right."

"Come and see."

He led them into the palatial stables where the horses were standing quietly in their stalls with plenty of food and water to hand. Iolo was just finishing grooming the last pack pony and grinned happily at Hywel as they approached.

"Isn't this great, sir!" he burst out with no sign of a stammer. "It's much better than I ever imagined. I needn't have been frightened at all! We've just got to clean the tack and then there's a feast for us - Lord Modron's grooms have fixed it - and they helped us groom the horses too."

The older grooms were already working on the tack and they grinned at the boy's enthusiasm.

"How's Mellt?" Hywel asked as they moved across towards him. He did not really need to ask as he and Saeth were standing gleaming in adjacent stalls.

"He's fine, sir, quite well behaved, and not really tired at all. I think he enjoyed the journey."

Duach and Hywel spent some time with their horses and then went to find a private spot for their doctoring. The liniment stung like fire and they did indeed yelp as they rubbed it in.

"Wheww! That's strong stuff," gasped Duach "Smells too."

"Uggh!" Hywel groaned. "My grandmother always says that the more it hurts, the more good it does. This must be doing a marvellous job. ... Ouch! ... That's enough. Let's go exploring."

They started walking around the outside of the plateau but, after a quick look, they stayed well away from the edge which dropped down in vertical cliffs for at least ten metres and then steeply again below that.

"No wonder they haven't got a fence," said Duach. "You don't need it with cliffs like that. I reckon that this is the strongest llys I've ever seen."

"Yes," Hywel replied thoughtfully. "Some of the sea forts have equally steep cliffs but they protect much less land and none of them have anchorages like that one down there. How many ships can you count?"

"Eight, no nine, on this side of the river with a dozen or so coracles on the other bank. Most of ships are not very big though, less than half the size of your father's."

"See the front one?"

"Yes, it's not the same as the others, is it?"

"No," Hywel said thoughtfully. "I don't think it's a trader. Can you see? It's got a mast but it also seems to have holes along the side, probably for oars. I need to get a closer look at it, but we don't have time tonight."

A noisy group of warriors of about their own age was standing in a circle on the grass and they wandered over to join them. Two of warriors were wrestling in the centre and the others were cheering on their favourite and betting heavily. The wrestlers were very evenly matched and they watched with interest.

"Who are they?" Hywel asked a tall, well-dressed youngster standing next to him.

"The red-haired one is Irish, I don't know his name, and the other is my friend Meurig. We live here."

There was a huge roar as Meurig managed to throw his opponent and get an immobilising arm lock on him. The Irish boy signalled surrender and the group broke up to sort out their winnings.

Hywel's neighbour introduced himself with a smile.

"Hello, I'm Huw ap Modron and you are welcome here."

"I'm Hywel ap Owain and this is Duach ap Bedwyr and we are here with Lord Rhys. We've just arrived and we haven't met anyone yet."

"Ah! The clots from Cemaes," said a sneering voice from behind them.

Hywel whipped round in fury.

"And who are you?" he demanded of a big, lumpish, fair-haired boy of about sixteen.

"Don't you know? ... So you're the clueless clots from Cemaes."

Hywel's fists bunched and he took a step forward only to be stopped by Duach's hand on his right arm and Huw's on his left.

"He's Caradog, the king's grandson," explained Huw apologetically.

"King's grandson or not," Hywel spat at Caradog. "Mind your manners."

"So, what are you going to do about it?"

Ram my fist into your face, Hywel wanted to say, but his father's threat flooded into his mind.

"Ignore you until you've grown up a bit," he said, and turned away.

"You insolent brat ... come here!" Hywel ignored him and kept walking. Fortunately, he was saved by the supper horn that sounded just at that moment. Huw took his chance and started shepherding the rest towards the hall and this broke up the incident.

"Hywel, you fool!" hissed Duach in a whisper. "That was just what he wanted. You've given the king an opportunity to get at Lord Rhys."

"I know," he forced out through clenched teeth. "I'd better tell him immediately." They ran across to their house but the two lords had already left for the hall. Hywel stood, irresolute. He would have to talk to him in his mind.

"Lord, may I speak to you?"

"Yes, Hywel, but be quick."

"I've just insulted the king's grandson and he's furious with me. I'm sorry."

"See me when I get back to the house."

"Yes, lord."

Hywel and Duach found seats right at the bottom of the hall, as far away from the high table as they could get. They were both hungry and started on the excellent food that was laid out before them. They both chose water to drink.

"I'm sticking to water at all future feasts," said Duach virtuously. "I hated how I felt after the last one. You've still got that treat in store."

"Yes."

"Oh look! ... There's Gwain, lord of Emlyn, sitting next to my father. I wonder if he's brought Cei with him. ... He should be down this end somewhere. ... Yes, there he is. ... You know Cei, don't you? He stayed with me last year."

Hywel kept his eyes on his plate and felt horrible. If his father had not frightened him before he left home, he would have got into a fight with the king's grandson, and what would that have done to Lord Rhys? Where was his judgement? His sense? He was supposed to be a councillor. He was so ashamed of himself that he just wanted to go outside and cry his eyes out like a child. Duach poked him in the ribs, hard.

"Come on, Hywel! It's not the end of the world. Rhys will forgive you - eventually. And aren't you supposed to be doing a job for him?"

He had even forgotten that!

"Thanks, Duach," he muttered ungraciously. "I'm better now and I'll start work."

Hywel started with the redheaded noble who had been with the king when they arrived and he struck gold immediately. He was Irish and staying with the king. They were planning something together against Rhys. No. His thought was not that clear. Something against Cemaes but Hywel couldn't make out what; he needed to find out more about the Irishman so that he could direct his thoughts towards what he wanted to know.

Next Hywel tried the lord of Pebidiog who ruled the coastal cantref to the south west of Cemaes. He wasn't thinking of anything in particular at the moment, just that he liked Modron's wine. He was happily relaxed and Hywel half expected him to start singing. His colleagues from the cantrefs of Rhos, Penfro and Gwarthaf were in the same state but the last one was a miserable man and was more likely to start fighting than singing. Hywel slid through a range of nobles and got absolutely nothing of value - obviously, most people did not think during a feast. He would have to wait until the conference started tomorrow to get anything useful.

Hywel also checked the small fry and they all turned out to be absolutely harmless. All, that is, except one - Pebyn! Hywel's archenemy was sitting four places to his right and he could not see him very well but there was no mistake. Pebyn as ever was. Hywel nudged Duach.

"Look three places to your right."

"It's sloppy, slimy Pebyn!" he whispered in amazement. "What's he doing here?"

"Emrys said that he's been semi-adopted by an Irish chief so, presumably, he's with the red-headed man we saw with the king."

"He's thick enough with the king's grandson anyway - just look at them!"

Duach was right. As they watched, Caradog put his arm across Pebyn's shoulder and leant across him to reach a jug of ale. Hywel did not like that combination at all. Pebyn's spite and Caradog's position spelled trouble - probably for him!

He slipped out of the hall unobtrusively and went to wait in the house. He fell asleep while he was waiting and only woke when Duach shook him after he followed Rhys into the room. Hywel scrambled to his feet and waited for retribution to fall.

"Ah! Hywel," said Rhys, with a yawn. "Did you find out anything useful tonight at the feast?"

Hywel gulped.

"Only that the king and the Irish chief are plotting something against Cemaes, lord. Not you personally, but the cantref. I couldn't work out what they were plotting but I should be able to get more tomorrow."

"Thank you. The conference is planned for mid-morning so get off to bed now and do not snore."

Hywel stared at him open-mouthed.

"What is wrong, boy? ... Oh, the king's grandson. ... I expected more self-control from a councillor but I am sure that you are thoroughly ashamed of yourself. Think before you speak in future. ... Goodnight."

"Thank you, lord. Goodnight." He went to his pallet in Rhys' room in a complete daze of disbelief and fell asleep immediately.

The boys were both up and out of the way before the two nobles got out of bed the next morning. Duach lingered over his breakfast but Hywel wandered outside into the cold, fresh air. To his surprise, Iolo was waiting for him.

"Sir, I was in the stables, looking at the horses at the far end - where the king's horses are," he explained. "Then a group of young warriors came in and started fooling around. They went down towards Mellt and I ran round the back, fast, and hid behind his stall. Then they started talking about you, sir. A big, flabby one with long black hair and a spotty face really bad-mouthed you. He also said that you were a Roman spy - and the others believed him! He was dressed in a funny coloured tunic. Another one, who wore a torc and seemed to be their leader, wants to teach you a lesson for something you did yesterday. They are planning to ambush you when you are on your way to some races that are going to be held this afternoon. He wants his friends to give you a good hiding but, for some reason, he can't get involved himself. I waited until they left the stables and then came to tell you. Is that all right?"

"Thank you, Iolo. That's very well done and I needed to know quickly." Hywel replied. "The flabby one is called Pebyn - he hates me and he tried to murder me once. Their leader, the one with the torc, is Caradog, the king's grandson, and I was rude to him yesterday. Don't worry about the ambush. I'll take care of that."

Hywel looked at his groom thoughtfully. Intelligent, discreet... yes. He'd do fine.

"Hang on here a moment, would you?" He went back into the house and got permission from Rhys to go down to the river to have a quick look at the ship that had intrigued him yesterday. Rhys agreed that Duach should stay close to the house to fetch him if the conference started early.

Hywel rejoined Iolo and grinned at him.

"I am a spy, Iolo, but my loyalty is to Lord Rhys and nobody else. It's a great secret and nobody must know except Duach. .... Would you like to become my apprentice?"

Iolo's eyes nearly popped out of his head.

"An apprentice spy? You really mean it?" Hywel nodded. "Then, yes, please! When do we start?"

"Right now - with a peculiar ship. Come on!"

The ship was about twelve metres long, which made it some two-thirds the size of their own, but in most other respects it was similar. It had a high bow and stern to cope with big waves, and the decks forward and aft were also set high. Most unusually, there were six holes midships on each side and Hywel was examining one of these closely when the watchman challenged him.

"I'm sorry, sir," he replied. "I meant no harm. But my father is a shipmaster and we don't have holes like these in any of our ships. What do you use them for? Oars?"

"Yes. Our captain wants to see you. Will you come on board?"

Iolo followed close at Hywel's heels as they were led to a small cabin at the stern where a squat, bearded man made them welcome. He told them that his grandfather had told him that his family was descended from a group of the Veneti tribe who were driven out of Gaul by Julius Caesar when the Roman army was 'pacifying' their country and settled in the south of Ireland. The Veneti had been masters of the Narrow Sea since time before time but the Romans had beaten them with ships that used both sails and oars. Ever since, his family had been trying to develop similar ships and this was the latest model.

"It's very difficult, you see, Hywel. Our ships are too heavy to be moved by the number of oarsmen we can carry, but, if we make them lighter, they can't cope with the sea. We are still trying to get the balance right and this is a trial voyage. Once our lord has finished his business with your king, we plan to explore your coast up to the Afon Teifi before turning for home. It's getting a bit late in the season but we need some moderately bad weather to test the ship."

"Whereabouts do you come from, sir? We have trading connections with Wexford."

"We are the kingdom to the west of it and we operate out of Waterford. Come and see us in the spring and I'll show you our other ships."

"Thank you, I'd like that very much. But I'm afraid that we have to get back now. Goodbye."

Hywel's mind was seething. That captain's thoughts had been quite clear - they were trying to built war boats. The next thing he needed to find out was the name of their chosen opponents. It couldn't be the Romans; there weren't any near enough. It was much more likely to be their neighbours and his interest in the Teifi suggested that it might be Cemais. But where did the king fit into all this? Hywel was very puzzled as he ran back to the llys with Iolo and then perched on a bench.

"Iolo, that ship is built for war and I'd like to know more about it. Or rather, I'd like to know more about what the Irish lord intends to do with it. He is not here by accident or on a purely social visit. He's planning something with the king and I'd like to know if anyone else is involved. He won't be coming to the conference this morning and it would be an ideal time for him to talk to other people. I'd like you to watch him for me, without being noticed yourself, and to note carefully anyone he meets. Will you do that for me?"

"Of course, sir!"

"He is a big, red-headed man who swaggers around as though he owns the place. He's wearing a lot of gold jewellery including the most magnificent dagger you've ever seen. We'll go and find him in a moment but stick to him until just before supper, if you can, and then come and find me. Come earlier if you lose him. Tell the horsemaster that you are doing a special job for me but not what it is - all right?"

Iolo nodded vigorously.

"But, sir. What about those other warriors - the ones that are going to ambush you? Couldn't I help with them?"

"No, I'll fix them! And I'll enjoy it too. You keep an eye on the Irishman for me. That's much more important. ... Just a moment." Hywel went into the house and found everything peaceful. Gwain of Emlyn was talking quietly with Rhys and Duach was playing fidchel, a sort of chess, in the corner with his friend Cei. He left them to it and went off with Iolo to find the Irishman.

A man came stomping out of the hall as they approached it, obviously furious about something, and he was followed a few moments later by a worried-looking Huw and his friend Meurig.

"What's wrong with him?" Hywel asked, pointing to the departing warrior.

"He's the envoy from Gwent and he's furious with the king," replied Huw. "I only hope that he doesn't carry out his threat and start for home."

"There's Anwyl, the king's nephew, going after him," said Meurig. "He'll talk him out of it."

"What's the king done?" asked Hywel.

"Cancelled this morning's meeting to go and visit the Irish ship," said Huw, with a laugh. "A two minute job that he could have fitted in this afternoon. But, no, it had to be done this morning, so the rest of the lords will have to kick their heels and wait. My father is trying to fix up some hunting but it's a bit late in the day and we'll only have a couple of hours. The races that the warriors of the escorts had arranged for this afternoon will have to be postponed until tomorrow because we'll be at the meeting and won't be able to watch them. Who'd host a king?" He grinned ruefully and shrugged his shoulders. Then he turned to Iolo.

"Hello, youngster. I'm Huw ap Modron and you are welcome here."

"I ... I'm Iolo ap Eliud, lord," stuttered Iolo flushing scarlet.

"Iolo's here as my groom but he's really my friend," Hywel explained. "We've just been down to look at this famous ship. It's impressive."

"Huw! The king's coming!" said Meurig urgently. "Let's get out of sight!"

The four of them drew back into the shadow of the doorway of the hall and watched. The Irishman rode beside the king and they were followed by the lords of Gwarthaf and Pebidiog with a very harassed-looking Modron bringing up the rear, leading his horse and talking animatedly to his steward. The man turned back as Modron mounted and clattered after the rest of the party.

"The wretched meeting is on again, Lord Huw," he said, "immediately after lunch. Your father asks that you tell the other lords while I make the arrangements."

"I don't think that I'd follow this king into battle!" laughed Huw. "Would you tell Lord Rhys, please, Hywel? I'll tell the others."

"Gwain of Emlyn is with him. I'll tell him too. See you later."

"Why does the king change his mind so much, sir?" whispered Iolo as they walked back across the grass.

"Only the gods know, Iolo," Hywel said with a grin. "But keep an eye on that Irishman for me when he gets back. ... And Iolo." He turned enquiringly. "You can't call me 'sir' if you're my friend - try Hywel - remember?"

"Yes ... Sir Hywel." Hywel threw a mock punch at him and he ran off laughing.

Hywel found the meeting later that morning quite interesting. He followed Rhys into the hall, carrying his shield, which was made of bronze and extremely heavy. Rhys took his seat at the table and Hywel stood against the wall behind him. Caradog carried the king's shield, Huw his father's and Cei the Lord of Emlyn's. Hywel had not met the other four shield-bearers yet. The king started the meeting by introducing the envoy and inviting him to talk about the Romans.

The envoy bowed.

"My lords," he started, "I have been sent by my master, the king of Gwent, to tell you about the fantastic opportunity we have to strike a severe blow against the Romans in the spring. As you know, the traditional boundary between my tribe, the Silures, and our eastern neighbours runs along the course of the Afon Gwy and the Mynydd Du. The Romans have broken this boundary in strength. They have established forts at Y Gelli Gandryll, they call that one Clyro, and at Usk, they call that one Burrium, and they have set up an iron industry around Trefynwy. We have fought them hard and we have caused them considerable damage but we have not been able to stop them taking away our land. But now we have heard that a lot of their soldiers have been withdrawn and their strength along our border is significantly reduced. My king thinks that this gives us an ideal opportunity to hit back but we need more men. Will you help us?"

"I support this request for help by the Silures," said the king, importantly. "And I would like each of you to provide one hundred warriors. What do you say?"

There was a stunned silence. Hywel did a quick gallop through the minds of the lords and laughed inside himself at the unanimous thought which, translated politely, said 'No.'

"Cemaes," said the king, "What do you say?" A sigh of relief came from the others.

"May I ask the envoy some questions first, sir?" asked Rhys politely.

"I can't see why," said the king. "But go ahead if you must."

"What exactly do you intend to do against the Romans? Are you trying to reclaim lands you have lost to them or are you just after loot?" asked Rhys.

"A bit of both, sir," replied the envoy with a grin. "Their weapons are worth having and their gold is even more useful. We intend to attack their supply columns and to starve the garrisons out of the forts. We will also attack as many other targets as we can so the Romans have to spread themselves thinly - which is where you come in. Also, we hope that our warriors who have been captured and are now Roman slaves will revolt and add to their problems."

"Where will you attack them first?"

"I don't know, sir. That will depend on the situation at the time. But they send regular supply columns to the forts and they should be pretty easy to ambush."

"Who will lead your forces?"

"Well, each tribe will have its own leader but one of our chiefs will be the overall commander as we have more experience of fighting the Romans than anyone else."

Rhys turned to the king.

"I have no more questions at the moment, sir."

"I have some, please," said the lord of Emlyn. The king nodded.

"What support have you been promised from other tribes?"

"We sent out envoys to all the kings at the same time, sir, so I don't know."

"When do you plan to assemble your troops?"

"In the first week of March. We will collect about half of them in the Mynydd Ddu north of Y Fenni and the rest in the hills west of the Wysg."

"What about supplies? Will you collect food or would we have to bring it with us?"

"We would expect you to bring three weeks food with you, sir. After that the Romans will feed us."

"Well said!" broke in the king. "Now, do you all agree?" There was much dubious head shaking and most of the lords refused to meet the king's eye. No one spoke and the silence lengthened until the king started to get restless and edgy. Finally, Rhys took pity on him.

"This is a serious matter, sir. I suggest that we have a break and take some time to consider it carefully."

"Oh! Very well," said the king, petulantly. "I will send a messenger when I want you back. You may go." The king glared at Rhys and his thoughts reflected the expression on his face with an unspoken addition - *'I'll get troops out of you if it kills me!'*

Hywel left the hall with a group of shield-bearers to find the Irish chief outside, exchanging banter with a couple of local lords. He was just about to pass behind him when he turned and spoke. Hywel slid into his mind immediately.

"Boy!"

"Yes, sir?"

"I understand that you visited my ship this morning." His thoughts were both suspicious and hostile.

"Yes, sir."

"My captain says that your father is a ship owner and that you trade with Wexford. Do you know Tegwyn ap Meredith?" His thoughts shocked Hywel and he had great difficulty in keeping his face blank. The Irishman hated uncle Tegwyn with a fierce and burning intensity and he was determined to kill him. Hywel wondered why because they could never have met - Tegwyn never left the cantref and the Irishman had not visited it.

"Yes, sir. My father is a ship owner; we trade with Wexford; and Tegwyn ap Meredith is my uncle. May I ask why you want to know?"

The Irishman smiled but the hatred showed in his eyes.

"I've heard great things of your uncle, boy. He helped my neighbours with food and weapons when they were losing a war four years ago. He also transported warriors from your cantref to help them fight back. As a result of his actions, my neighbours were able to save themselves and they have since regained much of their power." Hywel suddenly realised that the redhead had been their opponent. No wonder he hated Tegwyn!

He smiled at Irishman, as though he had taken his compliment at face value.

"Wexford was very badly damaged and we were glad to help, sir."

The Irishman nodded and turned away. Hywel saw Iolo appear from behind a pile of stacked wood and head in the general direction of the stables. His sandal gave him trouble in the middle of the open space and he bent to adjust it. He was doing a magnificent job and he didn't look directly at the Irishman once. Hywel realised that his own knees were shaking so he took a few deep breaths to steady himself before going back to the house.

Rhys was in the middle of a noisy discussion with Bedwyr, Gwain and Modron as Hywel passed through the hall of the house to take the shield to his room. He caught Hywel's eye.

"It would be better if we spoke, lord," Hywel said into his mind. Rhys nodded and joined him a few moments later. Hywel told him of the development of the war-boat and the loathing that the Irish chief had for his own family and then that the king was determined to get troops from Cemaes.

"Those are the facts, lord. But I have a most uncomfortable feeling. It isn't as strong as a thought and I do wish that Druid Mabon were here to guide me. But I think that the king wants to weaken you so that the Irish chief can attack us in the spring with less opposition. Would that be possible?"

"Yes, Hywel. Perfectly possible," he replied gravely. "Can you get me more information?"

"I hope so, lord, but I'm not sure. None of the other chiefs have anything interesting except that Lord Modron wishes the king in the Otherworld. I've got my groom watching the Irishman to see if he talks to anyone else and, if he does, I'll check them out carefully too. ... May I talk to Druid Mabon? I'd be much more comfortable with his guidance."

"Try it if you like, but do not be surprised if he bites your head off! ... Thank you, Hywel, you have done well."

Rhys left and Hywel lay on his pallet while he sent a very tentative thought to the druid. His response was vitriolic and Hywel withdrew his mind hastily. So, he was on his own. What else should he do? ... He drifted off to sleep while he was thinking about it.

Duach woke him with the news that Iolo wanted to see him and that it was nearly time for supper. Hywel felt horrible - all muzzy - and he stuck his head in a bucket of water to try and clear it. It did not really work and he was still half-asleep when he went out to see Iolo. They sat on the outside bench while Iolo described his adventures.

"I watched the Irishman, as you said, and it was quite boring. He spent a lot of time in his own house where he was visited by the advisors who came with the lords of Pebidiog and Rhos - not together but separately. The man from Rhos didn't stay long and looked furious when he came out. The other one stayed for ages and had a smug sort of look on his face when he came out. Then the king's nephew came and the Irishman left with him almost immediately. I followed them into the hall, carrying a couple of logs that I put on the fire, and they disappeared into a corridor at the back. I had just started to follow them there when a servant saw me and chased me out. The Irishman hasn't come out yet."

"That's great, Iolo, you almost qualify as a super-spy! You didn't happen to overhear any of his talk did you?"

Iolo grinned.

"He's staying in a round-house, sir, with a wattle and daub wall. I managed to get under the overhang of the roof and that gave me a hidden tunnel all the way round the building. I'm afraid that there's a bit of a hole in the wall now; they don't build very strongly here and my knife is sharp!"

"Very clever - but did you hear anything?"

"Not very much, but the Irishman gave the man from Pebidiog money. His first offer wasn't enough and they raised their voices as they argued about it. I'm afraid that I couldn't catch the reason for the bribe. They whispered that bit."

"Iolo, you are absolutely brilliant! You've got me just the information that I needed. You don't need to watch the Irishman tomorrow - he doesn't need to bribe anyone else, if my suspicions are correct." Hywel looked at him thoughtfully. "Iolo, may I ask you a personal question?"

"Of course, sir."

Hywel hesitated. …

"Your stammer. You haven't stammered once since we started talking but sometimes it's so bad you can hardly speak."

"I know. It's horrible. Sometimes people frighten me so much that my tongue won't work. And the harder I try the worse it gets."

"So I don't frighten you now?"

Iolo's smile split his face.

"Not at all. I was terrified of you when we first met because I thought that you wouldn't want me. But now that you've made me an apprentice spy, you obviously trust me and I'm happy so I don't stutter."

"Iolo, you're an idiot! But a good and useful idiot. Go and get your supper now, and thank you very much."

Hywel watched the man from Pebidiog during his own supper and fed the thought of gold into his mind. His thoughts turned into a mine of gold. He was very happy with the deal that he had done - so much gold for just turning a blind eye to any Irish ships that used the anchorage off Solva as a rendezvous in the spring. Some of the gold would have to go to the local headman, but not much because he would not understand the real value of the information. Then he started to daydream. The Irishman would never know if he told Lord Rhys that an attack was planned for the spring. He could do it discretely and Rhys was one of the most close-mouthed men he knew. He might pay well too ... Was it worth it?

Hywel left him arguing with himself and concentrated on his supper until the bard started to play. He was very good and his voice filled the hall, both when he sang and when he told stories. Then he started to play songs that warriors like to sing and the noise of the singing nearly lifted the roof off. Hywel was just reaching for a high note when his voice dropped to a low growl. Duach heard it and laughed.

"So your voice has broken at last! Thank the gods for that - your squeaking has been an embarrassment ever since we finished the warrior tests."

"Come on, grandfather! Yours only went a month ago so you can't crow too loud. ... I wonder if I'll still be able to sing when it settles down?"

"You can't sing now anyway, so it doesn't matter," said Hywel's kind, considerate and courteous friend, and, on that note, they took themselves off to bed.

Hywel was full of fidgets when he got up in the morning so he went round to the stable to collect Mellt with the intention of riding them off. Mellt seemed pleased to see him and played up until they got across the llys bridges and onto the good grass beyond. They rode around for the best part of an hour before Hywel turned back, reluctantly, to face another day as a shield-bearer. They were cantering through woodland a few kilometres from the llys when three horsemen appeared, lined up across the path ahead. Hywel had forgotten the threat of an ambush and lost his temper at such childish stupidity. He kicked Mellt into a gallop and he charged straight at them. Hywel was sure that they would not stand in the face of a determined attack but he screamed out his war cry, just to make certain.

"Keeeeeeeee ... Maes! ... Keeeeeeeee ... Maes! ... Keeeeeeeee ... Maes!" It worked like a charm and they scattered as Mellt thundered through them. To Hywel's amazement, the chant came back to him!

"Keeeeeeeee ... Maes! ... Keeeeeeeee ... Maes! ... Keeeeeeeee ... Maes!" A grinning warband rode out of the trees, followed by Iolo, and surrounded the three bullies. He managed to persuade an excited Mellt to slow down and turn back - eventually.

"What do you want us to do with this lot, Hywel?" asked the warband leader as he rode up. "Strip them, take their horses and let them walk home naked? And perhaps rough them up a bit first?"

"That sounds like a good idea." He sat looking at the scared youngsters for a long moment before speaking directly to them.

"I'm very tempted to let that happen and I will do so if you try anything as stupid as this again. Tell Caradog to get off my back and to stay off it. Understand?" They nodded sullenly.

"You may go." They rode off without saying a word.

"Nice one, Hywel," said the senior warrior. "You would have started a feud if you'd taken my suggestion - I only made it to scare them. But that was fun. We're bored out of our minds, just hanging around waiting and holding small races against the other cantrefs. We're off exploring now but we'll be back in time for the big races planned for this afternoon. Want to come?"

"I'd love to but I need to get back, and fast too. Thanks for your help. Goodbye."

Iolo followed Hywel back towards the llys at an easy canter. He was grinning from ear to ear.

"What am I going to do with you, Iolo?" Hywel said in exasperation. "I don't need a nursemaid!"

"It seemed like a good idea at the time, sir," he said, not a bit abashed. "I saw them collect their horses, followed them to find out where they were going to wait for you, and then went to fetch the warband. No trouble at all."

"But I could have dealt with them myself - they were only kids!"

"Kids or not, sir, they were all bigger than you, and there were three of them."

"No problem at all to a man of my calibre, particularly with you as my secret weapon! Thanks."

Iolo gave an elaborate salute and grinned even wider. Hywel had a sudden thought and slowed down.

"Iolo? Did you see anyone else in the stables?"

"No. Just the three of them."

Hywel grunted his thanks. So Pebyn was still a coward and too scared to face him. He would tackle him later.

CHAPTER 6 – TREASON

The house was horribly quiet and empty as Hywel entered. Aled came in from the kitchen to greet him and grinned as he saw the expression on his face.

"It's all right, master Hywel. You haven't missed the meeting. That's planned for noon."

"Thank the gods for that! I was getting worried! Where is everyone?"

"The two lords are with Gwain of Emlyn and Duach has gone off to see a girl," he said with a straight face.

"Duach? ... A girl?" said Hywel in amazement.

"Well, it was really master Cei who wanted to see the girl and Duach went along to keep him company. ... The girl is Nest, Lord Modron's daughter, and I gather that her eyes are a deeper blue than the sea; her hair is blacker than a raven's wing; her skin is whiter than hawthorn blossom; and her lips are redder than holly berries.... I am quoting master Cei precisely but I cannot vouch for the accuracy of his statements." Aled kept his expression neutral.

"You don't believe that drivel, do you, Aled?"

He grinned.

"Master Cei is normally quite truthful but you may wish to check it for yourself. I understand that she spends much of her time in the garden behind the hall."

Hywel hesitated. He didn't feel like playing his flute and there was not anything else to do so he might as well go and join the others.

"Thanks, Aled. I'll go and inspect this paragon and I'll let you know if there's any truth in Cei's ramblings!"

There was a large group of young people in the garden, about four girls and at least three times as many boys, including Caradog and Pebyn. Cei and Duach were sitting on the grass on the outside of the group and Hywel sat down beside them. Cei was looking utterly miserable and Duach was looking utterly bored. He turned to Hywel with relief.

"Hi, Hywel. Am I glad to see you! This idiot thinks that the world has come to an end because Nest is too busy talking to Caradog to take any notice of him. Tell him not to be such a fool."

"I'm in love, Hywel," said Cei. "I adore her, every bit of her right down to the tips of her toes. Have you ever seen anyone more beautiful?"

"Yes, my aunt Catrin who lives in Ireland. Nest is pretty enough but she's still a child and anyone who is impressed by Caradog is a fool."

"Are you calling her a fool?" He scrambled to his feet and stood over Hywel with his fists clenched.

"Yes, I am. But we can't fight here; it wouldn't be polite to the lady. Let's go behind the stables and then you can use your fists to teach me how wrong I am." He winked at Duach as he got up and followed Cei.

Duach started giggling and went red in the face trying to hide it. They reached the back of the stables and Hywel had no difficulty in avoiding Cei's first furious onslaught and tripping him up. He and Duach promptly sat on top of Cei and tried to make him see sense. They were unsuccessful.

"What you say might be true, but I don't care - I'm in love! ... I'm going back. She might even smile at me this time."

"He's a fool," said Duach as they watched Cei hurry off. "I've never seen a sensible person change so fast. It's unbelievable!"

"Maybe he's been got at by the fairies, the Tylwyth Teg. Bard Emrys says that their spells can be broken by striking the affected person with iron and, in difficult cases, it needs to be done three times. Shall we try it?"

"Why not? We've nothing to lose and you have to try and help a friend."

That triggered the thoughts that Hywel had been trying not to think. What was he going to do about his Roman friend - help him or abandon him?

"Duach, say you had two friends who were enemies of each other, which one would you support?"

"That's a nasty one. ... I don't know. ... The one you have known the longest, maybe, or perhaps the one you are closest to. ... Maybe you shouldn't support either but try to make them friends with each other. ... Why do you ask?"

"Well, the Silures, who are fellow Britons, want to attack my Roman friend in Gloucester using warriors from Cemaes. Fellow Britons may not classify as friends but warriors from Cemaes certainly do."

"Ah! ... I see the problem. What does Lord Rhys think?"

"He's uncertain too. But, although I would value his opinion, I think that I should make up my own mind because the Roman is my friend, not his."

"Well, you've got time to think and, from what my father said this morning, it's by no means certain that Rhys will agree to lend warriors to the Silures."

"Let's go and find out. The conference should be starting soon."

The meeting started quite normally with the king giving a summary of the Silures' request and repeating that he wanted a hundred warriors from each cantref. There was some discussion and six of the chiefs agreed to provide twenty men each. The king was furious but nothing he said altered their minds - that was their final offer. Rhys remained silent throughout the discussion until the king challenged him directly. Hywel slipped into the king's mind as Rhys started to reply.

"I am expecting an attack from the Irish in the spring, sir, and I cannot spare any warriors until I have defeated it," he said calmly but firmly. The king was amazed that he was so positive and wondered how on earth he had found out.

"You swore allegiance to me!" shouted the king. "And that means providing warriors when I need them."

"I am not refusing to provide warriors - I would provide them immediately if I thought that you really needed them but you do not - whereas I need all my own men because I am sure that Cemaes is under threat. I would advise all the other coastal cantrefs to take similar precautions too. Once I have dealt with that threat I will consider the request from the Silures."

"Prove it!" shouted the king. "Prove that the Irish are planning to attack you in the spring!"

Rhys looked at him scornfully.

"You know that I can not prove it! I have very good reason to believe that such an attack is coming and that is enough for me. Will you provide warriors to support me when they arrive? If you do, and we defeat the Irish, I will provide double your number to support the Silures."

"Cemaes?" said the lord of Pebediog uneasily. "Am I vulnerable too?"

"Yes," replied Rhys shortly. "I'll send one of my advisors to discuss it with you. Perhaps we can make some useful joint arrangements - but maybe the king might like to take the lead?"

"No way!" replied the king. "You are talking rubbish! The Irish haven't attacked us for ages. They are our friends - talk to the chief who is here at the moment!"

Hywel fought to keep his face straight as the giggles built up inside him. He did not dare look at Duach.

"Yes," said Rhys dryly. "But I believe that they are a greater threat to us than the Romans are and I also believe that the Silures are heading for disaster. They have no clear aim, except collecting loot, and their lack of administrative planning is pathetic. The Romans are immensely strong, despite the withdrawal of one legion. They can move troops rapidly to reinforce threatened areas and their supply system is superb. I believe that you would be wise to negotiate with them instead of fighting them. We could almost certainly get an agreement that would permit us to run our own affairs as an allied state, like the Brigantes, and this would be infinitely preferable to constant warfare leading to eventual defeat.

"The sooner we start to negotiate this agreement the better. We will get much better terms if we start discussions now rather than waiting until the legions are on the move against us."

This was close to treason and the king was flabbergasted. The other chiefs had mixed reactions. Rhys and Bedwyr had talked to them, and to the king's nephew, Anwyl, outside the formal conference sessions but, obviously, the idea was new to the king.

"How strong are the Romans?" asked Anwyl.

"Well, they have three legions left in Britain and each legion has about 5,000 heavily armed foot soldiers and 120 cavalry together with engineers, artillery and support troops. They also have several thousand auxiliary troops attached to them. These generally have lighter armour. There are also independent auxiliary units of 500 - 1,000 men, both infantry and cavalry. But their main strength is not in their large numbers but in the speed with which they can move troops from one threatened area to another. The main legions can cover over 20 Roman miles or 30 kilometres in five hours."

"You are remarkably well informed," sneered Anwyl. "How do you know all this? There aren't any Romans anywhere near you. Are you making it up?"

"My information is accurate," snapped Rhys.

"I've heard that one of your warriors is in the pay of the Romans," said Anwyl. "Have they bought you too?"

Hywel was trying to monitor the king's mind and Anwyl's at the same time. It was difficult and he could not spare any time to react to the insult to his father.

'The king truly believes that you are a Roman sympathiser, lord,' he flashed to Lord Rhys. *'He got it from the Irish chief.'*

"That is too ludicrous an idea for me to bother to deny," said Rhys with icy politeness. "One of my warriors does indeed trade with the Romans and he is a valuable source of information. He is also totally loyal to me."

"Do you really think that the Romans would make a treaty with us?" asked Lord Modron.

"Yes," replied Rhys. "It would be to our mutual advantage. You may have noticed two things. Firstly, the commander who ordered the attack on Ynys Mon was replaced very quickly and, secondly, they have stayed within their current boundaries for the last four years. This suggests to me that, unless they are provoked by senseless attacks such as the Silures are proposing, they would be content to stay within them."

. "It makes sense," said Modron, nodding

"Sir," said the lord of Emlyn to the king, "It sounds like a very good idea. Could I suggest that we ask Lord Rhys to find out whether or not the Romans would be interested in such a treaty?"

The king looked as though he was going to have a seizure. His face was scarlet and his eyes were nearly popping out of his head with fury.

"I will not have it!" he shouted at Lord Rhys. "You are talking treason! You have given me good cause for removing you from your cantref."

He turned to Anwyl who was tugging at his sleeve. "And what do you want?"

Anwyl whispered in his ear. Hywel dived into his mind and opened up a simultaneous mind link with Lord Rhys.

'Take care, sir,' said Anwyl urgently. *'Don't take on Lord Rhys yet until you know that you have the support of the other lords. Emlyn and Deugleddyf will almost certainly side with him and you will need all the other four if you take any overt action against him. I'm not sure that Rhos will support you and Penfro will dither. Call a break and let me check with them.'*

'No,' whispered the king. *'I've got sufficient troops of my own here and there are also the Irishmen. I'll arrest him tonight and then the others won't be able to do anything. Don't argue!'*

The king turned and looked at the other lords, who had all been stretching their ears to catch the conversation, and then stared hard at Lord Rhys.

"Lord Rhys," he said slowly and formally. "I forbid you to contact the Romans and I forbid you to discuss this ridiculous idea with the other lords. I order you to produce warriors in the spring to support the Silures."

"I hear your orders, sir," said Rhys with a wry smile. "If you have nothing more for me, I bid you farewell. I leave this afternoon."

Rhys stood up, bowed to the king and made for the door with Hywel in close attendance. Bedwyr and Duach followed behind.

CHAPTER 7 – THE RETURN

Rhys started issuing orders as soon as they left the hall. Duach was sent flying to alert the horsemaster, to get his horse and to collect the leader of the warband. Bedwyr was sent to Lord Modron's steward and Aled was sent to start packing their possessions. Hywel was told to sit quietly in a corner and to monitor the king.

The king's mind was in chaos and he could not hold onto any thought for more than a few seconds. The meeting broke up almost immediately after the Cemaes party left and the king stamped off to his own apartments with Anwyl and his grandson. The grandson was sent running for the Irish chief and Anwyl was sent to sound out the other lords to see if they would lend the king their escorts to stop Rhys leaving.

Hywel left the king's mind and followed his nephew's instead as he was very curious to see what the other lords thought. The lords of Emlyn, Deugleddyf and Rhos replied that they intended to escort Lord Rhys to the safety of his own cantref. The lord of Gwarthaf said that he needed his escort as he was going home himself and the lords of Penfro and Pebediog refused to get involved on either side.

Hywel went back to the king just in time to catch the beginning of his discussion with the Irishman and he could not stop himself laughing out loud. Rhys turned to him in surprise and laughed too when he explained that the king and the Irishman were convinced the only way that Rhys could have discovered their plans was by bribing one of their people to spy on them and that they were each blaming the other for giving their plan away.

They didn't quite come to blows but they weren't far off it!

Rhys grinned and clapped Hywel on the shoulder.

"Well done, boy. You can stop monitoring him now. We are just about ready to leave. Go and collect your own gear or you will be left behind."

They set out like a wedding party and the cavalcade stretched for a couple of kilometres. Hywel and Duach rode with the Cemaes warriors at the front of the combined escort and, as soon as they reached relatively open ground, they were allowed to ride ahead with the forward scouts - Hywel went to the left and Duach to the right. It was great fun and they got to the foothills that marked the boundary of the cantref all too soon. They could see the border guard watching from the pass above and the boys turned and rode back to resume their duties as the close escort. To their surprise, the lord of Emlyn had decided to go all the way home with them and he brought his escort too. The rest turned back with waves and shouts of good wishes.

They reached the pass as dusk was falling and the border guard had a large peat fire burning to welcome them. They ate the superb supper that Modron's steward had provided and then Rhys called on Hywel to make music. He dug out his flute and soon the whole party was singing a mixture of martial songs, love songs and folk songs. They kept at it for ages until Hywel was absolutely exhausted and could play no more. He curled up in his cloak and fell into a dreamless sleep.

Just before dawn a rough tugging on his cloak woke him from a deep sleep. He stuck his head out for air and came face to face with Mellt who blew gently into his face. Hywel stared up at him in surprise, groaned, and then huddled down for the last few minutes of comfort. Mellt tugged at his cloak again, more insistently, moved away a few steps then looked back over his shoulder. He obviously wants me to do something, thought a groaning Hywel, as he clambered stiffly to his feet while yawning wide enough to break his jaw. He looked across the rough moorland to where Iolo was waiting with a bunch of grooms.

"Stupid horse," muttered Hywel. "Go back to Iolo." Mellt cantered off as Iolo and Hywel waved to each other.

The party made good time down from the pass and stayed on the main track as far as the standing stones near the small village at Ffynnon Fair where, after resting the horses and feeding the people it split into three. The Cemais warriors joined the lord of Emlyn and his men to escort them to their cantref. The remainder turned left for Nanhyfer. It seemed to be a tiny group now - even though it still totalled ten people and twelve horses.

Rhys turned to the two boys.

"Bedwyr and I are going to make our own way home, boys. I want you two to escort the servants and to make sure that they stay safe." He laughed at their crestfallen faces. "You have to pay for your fun sometime! Hywel, please would you tell your father that I would like to see both of you at the llys for a council meeting - mid-morning tomorrow - right?"

"Yes, lord," he muttered as Rhys rode off.

"Two of us," said Duach. "One in front and one behind?"

"I suppose so," replied Hywel. "But there's no real threat as long as we stay closed up. Can't we ride together?"

"No," Duach replied firmly. "And, for your un-warrior-like thought, you can bring up the rear. It shouldn't take long."

The rest of the journey did indeed pass quickly. It was the first time for ages that Hywel was effectively on his own with time to think. He had a fair amount to think about - being a man, being a councillor, and his general relationships with other people that had changed subtly. He now had to take responsibility not only for his own actions, but for Iolo's as well. But besides all that, he had a constant, nagging worry about what he was going to do about his Roman friend. His distaste and dislike for the king were colouring his thoughts and he needed to talk it over with his grandmother who would have a much more balanced view. Hywel had just reached this conclusion when, to his surprise, they stopped outside Duach's farm. Bedwyr was sitting on the bank of the river waiting for them.

"No enemies? No robbers? No monsters? All peaceful?"

"No, sir, nothing interesting," Hywel replied. "Sir, does Duach really need to come all the way to the llys with us? Can't he stay here with the rest of your party? It would be more sensible. I would die of surprise if there was anything hostile in the last couple of kilometres."

"You're right, Hywel, and, if the horsemaster agrees to lead a pack horse, you and your groom can take the short cut home ... What to you think Rhun?"

"No problem, lord," replied the horsemaster. "I'll shout rude words at anyone who frightens me." The idea of anything or anyone frightening such a cheerful, competent figure and the image of him shouting in fright, reduced the rest of them to helpless giggles. They parted with mutual good wishes and Hywel and Iolo got home about an hour later. Hywel left the horses to Iolo and went into the house to find the rest of his family.

He found his father and Tegwyn in the storeroom planning the range and number of goods that they wanted the craftsmen to make for them over the winter. They welcomed him warmly and took a break to hear all his news. They were fascinated by the Irish chief. Tegwyn thought that his hatred was very amusing and he flexed his muscles in pretended preparation for the fight. Owain was more thoughtful.

"Would you make a sketch the Irish ship for me, please Hywel, together with what dimensions you can remember. I'd like to see her, and to take Gryffydd with me, if she comes up this way, but Lord Rhys' blunt warning that he knows all about the project may cause them to cancel the whole thing - as no doubt he intended."

"I don't think that they'll cancel the whole thing, Father. You could have lit a fire from the rage and hatred that were coming off the Irishman towards uncle Tegwyn. He might be a bit more cautious but he'll still come. He's bound to have been fed a lot of information about us by Pebyn. Unfortunately, I didn't have time to question him. I might have been able to bully something useful out of him."

"I don't think that matters. The Irish chief wouldn't have told him anything important. ... It's an awful pity that it's too late in the year for us to go sailing," mused Owain. "I'd love to go and talk to the Veneti about fighting with ships. Gryffydd and I will have to think hard this winter. The Roman military ships you saw on one of your holidays in Gloucester were very different and the Veneti would know that. So this experimental ship is almost certainly aimed at us. ... But, you know, they would be fools to use it for an attack against us - it would be much too risky. If they have any sense they'll stick to their tried and tested longboats. ... Was there anything else?"

Hywel hesitated.

"Only one more thing, sir. ..."

Owain's eyebrows climbed up to his hairline at the 'sir'!

"Thank you for frightening me so badly before I left. I was about to start a fight with the king's grandson when your threat stopped me in my tracks. I would have embarrassed Lord Rhys seriously if I'd gone ahead - so, thank you."

"What on earth did you say to the poor boy, Owain?" demanded Tegwyn.

"Only that I'd confine him to an empty ship when he got back home if he was stupid."

"Nasty! I collected four or five sessions over the years from our father and once he 'forgot' to feed me for three days. That was when that girl in Crymych claimed that I promised to marry her and I hadn't. How many did you get?"

"About the same. On one session, I was down to eating whatever raw fish I could catch on a bit of string! ... So you be careful, young man. The threat is very real and there are two experts wielding it!"

Hywel was fascinated by this glimpse into family history. His grandfather must have been a frightening person but he sounded fun too. It was a great pity that Hywel had never met him but he was lost at sea before he was born.

Hywel left them and went to find his grandmother who was preparing medicines and salves from the herbs that she had grown during the summer. She made quite a fuss of him and then they sat down to talk through his confusion over matters of loyalty.

"Can I spell out my understanding first, please, Nan?" She nodded. "As I see it, the Silures are not really the problem - we don't know them and we owe them nothing. The real problem is our relationship with the king. I've sworn loyalty to Lord Rhys and that's easy - I respect him enormously and he would have my loyalty anyway. I haven't sworn anything to the king but Lord Rhys has. Does his oath bind me as well - because I don't like or trust the king? Even worse, the king is helping the Irishman to attack my family and our cantref. Doesn't that cancel any oath that Lord Rhys has made to him?"

"Ugh, Hywel! You are into politics, not loyalties. You are bound by any allegiance that Lord Rhys accepts. But, although he has sworn to support the king, he also has a loyalty to his cantref that, at times, can be more important. This is one of them. In his judgement, the threat to the cantref is greater than the threat to the kingdom. Theoretically, by refusing to provide warriors to the king he has broken his oath but think about what he actually said - he agreed to support the king after he made sure that the cantref was safe - so he has not actually broken it."

"Difficult, isn't it Nan? But if we're not sending warriors to the Silures anyway, there is no reason why I couldn't tell the Romans what they are doing."

"I think you are right, Hywel. Particularly as the Romans do not plan to attack anybody - they will only be defending themselves. It would be different if they were invading us. Then you would have a real conflict of loyalties "

His grandmother had made things a lot clearer but he couldn't ask her advice on the last question that bothered him. He really needed Druid Mabon who was not available. So, he would have to make up his own mind, thought Hywel, even if the end result led to his own banishment for treason and for disobeying the druid.

Hywel took Owain outside after breakfast so that he could talk to him privately about the decisions he had made during the last three days. Owain looked at him sympathetically as they settled onto the outside bench.

"Bad night?" he asked.

"Yes, Father. I haven't had much sleep for a couple of nights. ... I've decided to go to Gloucester overland."

"I thought that you might. You didn't want to discuss it with me first?" Hywel had been a bit worried about how he would react and he was relieved that Owain's tone was light and friendly.

"No. I'm sorry, but I felt that it had to be my own decision as Aulus is more my friend than yours and you were uncertain when we last spoke about it. I did talk it over with my grandmother."

"I was, and so were Lord Rhys and Druid Mabon. But I can see why you reached your decision and I agree with it. When do you intend to leave?"

"As soon as I can. The weather is reasonable now and I would like to be well on my way back before the snow sets in on the mountains for the winter. ... I plan to take Iolo with me. Can I borrow a decent horse for him?"

"Of course. ... You do realise that the Silures will think that you are a spy and a traitor and they will kill you if they find out what you're doing?"

"Yes, indeed. That's the main reason why I've decided not to take Duach with me. I've got a cover story that I reckon will be good enough to protect me but wouldn't really work for him. How about an apprentice bard with a broken voice going to visit his grandfather at Lydney - bardic proof provided by my flute? Bards are protected when they wander so we should be relatively safe and be able to get food and shelter quite easily."

"Not bad. ... And on the return journey?"

"Still an apprentice bard but I'm looking for my widowed mother who has married again, left Lydney and gone to live somewhere in Emlyn."

"Yes, ... I reckon that should work," Owain mused. "The only disadvantage is that you won't be able to carry a sword but that may not matter too much as you are still young enough to look inoffensive. How about clothes – bard's robes? And Mellt? He's a bit upmarket for an apprentice bard."

Hywel grinned.

"My master is rich and I'm taking Mellt as a present from him to a chief who lives near Trefynwy. Unfortunately, he will die before we get there and Mellt will have to come back with us. I think I will stick to ordinary clothes – bards robes are a bit obvious and apprentices don't wear them anyway."

Owain looked at him long and thoughtfully and then he grinned broadly.

"You know, Hywel, you haven't really got any earth-shattering news for Aulus although I'm sure that he will be pleased to see you. On the other hand, you could get a lot of very useful information for Lord Rhys, particularly on the Silures - their state of readiness, their dispositions, their morale - that sort of thing. During your time with Aulus, you could make a pretty good guess on whether or not the Silures could really hurt him; he might even tell you! So, I formally enrol you as a solo spy, on the normal rate of pay, and task you with discovering this information. You will be entirely on your own and, if anything goes wrong, we will not attempt to rescue you or to ransom you. Do you accept these conditions?"

"Yes, sir. Thank you very much," gulped Hywel.

"As a spy, you are permitted to lie to protect your identity and your mission – I cleared that with Mabon and Lord Rhys a long time ago but you are still bound by the warrior's code for everything else. I'd also like you to get a briefing from Cynan who lives at Crymych. He's retired now but he used to be the most brilliant spy in our network. Learn what you can from him - it could save your neck."

"I didn't know that he was a spy!"

"There is a lot you don't know, my clever son! Are you going to tell Lord Rhys today?"

"Yes, after the meeting."

"A word of advice, Hywel." The boy looked at his father inquiringly. "I know that you are a man now, and growing up fast, but don't just tell Lord Rhys that you are going to Gloucester. It would be much more tactful to ask his permission - he won't refuse you."

"I'm terribly sorry, Father. Is that what I did to you?" He nodded and grinned broadly and then hugged him.

"Come on. Let's get our cloaks and be off to the llys."

Lord Rhys looked at Hywel very thoughtfully when he submitted his proposal.

"I've no objection to you going, Hywel. In fact, I think that it is a good idea and any information you can bring back will be very useful. But, tell me, could you not send your Roman friend a message in his mind instead of travelling all that way? It would save you an awful lot of effort."

"There are two problems, lord. Firstly, I can only reach that sort of distance if I am talking to someone who also has mind skills or someone I know very well, like my grandmother. I have to be close to get into the mind of someone like the king or the Irish chief; I couldn't reach either of them from here. Druid Mabon might be able to do so as he is much more powerful than I am - and he is my second reason. He has threatened me with horrible penalties if I give away my secret to anyone without his permission and I dare not risk it. He won't talk to me until after Samhain and I can't afford to wait until then before starting out."

Lord Rhys grinned.

"Yes, he frightens me too. I've seen him do magic that has made my hair stand on end and I would never disobey a direct order from him! ... When do you leave?"

"In three or four days time, lord. ... I wonder if you could possibly help me?" He smiled and nodded. "You see, it's Duach. I don't want him to come with me because, as a pair, we would be too conspicuous and that would increase the danger significantly. He won't listen to that as an argument so ... please could you forbid him to come? He'll take notice of what you say."

"He does have a point, Hywel. Are you sure?"

"Yes, lord. Absolutely sure. I need to disappear into the background and I reckon that I can do that more easily with a humble young groom than with Duach. You've only got to look at him, and the way that he carries himself, to see that he is descended from your family and that his father is a lord."

"You have the same look yourself, boy!"

"Perhaps, but I have practised hard at being a trader and you've only got to grovel to a fool a couple of times to learn how to appear to be humble!"

"All right, I agree. Duach is forbidden to leave the cantref until after the midwinter solstice. You can bear my message to him - and the best of luck on your journey."

Hywel went straight to Duach's house and he was furious! He thought that the whole plan was stupid and that, instead, they should take Gwyn and Cei with them, go armed and fight off any opposition they met. He refused to accept that if they got into any fight at all they would have failed and would have to turn back. He didn't believe Hywel when he told him about Lord Rhys' order and he stormed away with the firm intention of going to the llys to get the order cancelled. Hywel was very depressed as he rode home slowly and he could only hope that this would not seriously damage their friendship.

CHAPTER 8 – THE SOLO SPY

Hywel went to see Cynan at Crymych early the next morning and took a whole pile of his grandmother's medicines and salves with him. Cynan had suffered from pains in his joints for a long time but last year the pain had become so bad that he had been forced to stop travelling. He greeted Hywel warmly from his chair by the fire and his wife came bustling in with food and drink for them. He watched Hywel quizzically until she left.

"So! Your father has recruited you, has he, young Hywel? He hasn't wasted any time!"

"How did you know, sir?" Hywel asked him in amazement. "Can you read minds?"

"No. Body language. But you gave yourself away badly there. You should keep your cover, even with other spies, until you have a reason for breaking it. ... Anyway, welcome to the Brotherhood. May the gods guide your tongue and give you the cloak of invisibility."

"Thank you, sir. I'm tasked with going to Gloucester, through Lydney, to collect information on the Silures and the Romans. My father thought that you could teach me enough to keep me alive."

Cynan laughed.

"I don't know about that. You've got enough wits to look after yourself and you've done a pretty good job on your trading voyages!" He grinned at Hywel's surprise. "Oh, yes. I know all about those. Your father and I share secrets and he's terribly proud of you. But there are some big differences between spying as a ship-borne trader and a land-based one. The ship provides you with a secure base and friends to talk to. If things start to get difficult, you just up anchor and sail away. On land, it's very different. You are completely on your own and the loneliness sears your soul. Every man, woman and child is your enemy and you have no easy escape if things go wrong - just hundreds of kilometres of hostile territory to cross as unobtrusively as you can. But for all that, it's the most exhilarating game you can imagine!"

"Exhilarating, sir?"

"Yes - pitting your wits against the world! There are two basic strategies. The easiest one is to fade into the background so that people don't notice you - I did that as a pedlar with a couple of pack horses - but it restricts the level of the information you have access to. The other one is to make yourself highly noticeable so that people can't believe that you are a spy - you did that when you made friends with a Roman general - and that gives you access to the highest quality information. The problem is that there aren't too many handy Roman generals!"

"I plan to be an apprentice bard with a broken voice going to see my grandfather. I have a step-grandfather who lives in Lydney which is why I have to go there first before going on to Gloucester."

"Sounds good and you need not be in a hurry so you can afford to take the easier low level route around the mountains - the big mountains to the east of the Afon Tywi are absolute killers from the end of this month to at least May or even June. You should be pretty safe until you reach Aberhonddu as the locals are friendly and stick to the old ways. They will instinctively protect a bard - even an apprentice one! But east of that, things could get very difficult. Let me think."

Hywel sat and watched pictures in the fire as Cynan seemed to argue with himself. Cynan had certainly given him a lot to think about but the exhilaration he had mentioned was markedly absent! Hywel was scared stiff!

"Has your father given you a code name yet?" Cynan asked suddenly.

"No, sir. Do I need one?"

"Of course. We are the Brotherhood of Seals and each of the brothers has a colour - it's useful both to identify yourself and to confirm messages. I was the Grey Seal and, as I'm going to give you details of some of my contacts, you had better be the Son of the Grey Seal. Your father will probably shorten it to the Son of the Seal - but stick to the grey for this journey."

"Yes, sir. It will be an honour." Hywel really meant it as, by transferring his name Cynan was also transferring part of his spirit and, hopefully, most of his luck!

"The first part of your journey is fairly easy, you just follow the Afon Teifi up to Llanbedr - take you maybe two days. Then you turn southeast on a well-used track to the gold mines at Dolaucothi. It's a fair climb and it gets worse until you get to the pass at Bwlchcefnsarth but then you drop down fast through a steep, heavily wooded valley until you reach the Afon Tywi. That valley used to scare the daylights out of me; there were monsters watching from behind every rock and the horses hated it.

"Keep this side of the river and go upstream until another big river joins it from the right. Stay with the Tywi but cross it where you can so that you are riding to the east of it. You'll soon come to yet another river joining from the right and that's the one you need to follow. This is a good place to stop for the night as the local chief, who lives on the high ground just ahead of you, is a man-mountain, tall, strong and immensely fat and he loves visitors. You may find it difficult to get away from him!

"The last river, the Gwydderig, will take you through the mountains up a steady slope that is just about right for pack animals but be prepared to camp out overnight as there aren't many hamlets up there. Keep going until you get to the small village of Trecastell. Here you pick up the Afon Wysg that is also called the Usk and follow it downhill to the big village of Aberhonddu. If, for any reason, you need to escape you can break to the north here - the Romans are only twenty kilometres away. The track runs alongside the river for about another seven kilometres and then it swings north to a place called Bwlch to avoid a deep gorge.

"Bwlch is a funny place, it's like a raised finger sticking into the land of the king of Gwent where your troubles really start. Go and make yourself known to the local chief, Idwal ap Merfyn, who lives in Castell Blaenllynfi and introduce yourself as my son. He saved my life once and he will be able to tell you more about the Silures than you would be able to discover in a month of feast days." ... He broke off as a spasm of pain crossed his face and his body jerked in his chair.

"I'm sorry, Hywel. Could you ask my wife for my medicine, please?"

Hywel sat quiet while she tended to him and he prayed to the gods that he would never suffer as Cynan did. He was about the same age as Owain but his body was bent and twisted like an old man's and his hair was completely white. The medicine started to take effect and his muscles relaxed. He groaned in relief.

"I need to finish quickly, Hywel, because the medicine sends me to sleep. ... Stay with the river to Y Fenni but be extremely cautious. The king lives in a llys to the south but one of his most aggressive chiefs has a fort on the outskirts of the village. You have to go through the village, your mission gives you no choice, but do take care - I want to see you back here sometime!

"Y Fenni marks the end of the big mountains and you leave the river Wysyg there and cross flattish land to Trefynwy which is on the River Gwy, which is also called the Wye. The Wye can be difficult to cross if there has been a lot of rain so, if the bridge at Trefynwy is closed, you are stuck until the water level goes down. Once you're over the Wye it's less than a day's ride to Lydney. Does that help?"

"It helps a lot, sir, thank you very much. I'll leave you to sleep now and I hope that my grandmother's medicines help you. Goodbye."

Hywel was reciting Cynan's directions to himself as he rode home when Bard Emrys' mind burst into his like a fresh breeze.

'Hi, Hywel, ... how are you doing and where are you?'

'I'm doing fine, thank you and I'm on my way home from Crymych. Why do you ask?'

'Well, Mabon's disappeared and I'm looking after his compound while he's away. Can you come and see me?'

'I'm awfully busy. Can't we just talk?'

'No. I need to see you in the all too solid flesh. I've got some lovely apples!'

'Oh ... very well! But I really am busy and I can't stay long'

Hywel was making fast time back towards Nanhyfer when, close to the hamlet of Crosswell, he heard the noise of group of men talking, laughing and making themselves agreeable to at least one girl. It sounded about ten men, or two warbands worth, which was a very large party on a quiet, peaceful autumn day. He had not heard that any special exercises were planned for the day so he decided to investigate.

There were a dozen or so warriors scattered around the hamlet, significantly outnumbering the locals. Most had taken off their weapons and were lounging at their ease, eating and drinking, but three or four of were pestering a pretty girl who obviously was not enjoying their attention.

"Come on my pretty," growled one of the warriors and grabbed her around the waist. "Give us a kiss then."

The girl screamed and fought him but he was too strong for her. Her father tried to rescue her and got punched unconscious for his pains. Hywel edged Mellt into the group and dragged the warrior off by his hair.

"Stop it, man! That girl doesn't want you. ... Who are you anyway?"

"What's with you?" demanded the warrior aggressively.

"I'm Hywel ap Owain. I'm a warrior of Cemais and I have every right to be here. You don't. Where are you from?"

My name is Padrick and I'm from Waterford. I'm here at the invitation of the boy behind you - Pebyn. We are going to stay with his family for a while."

Hywel's heart sank to his boots and he turned round slowly in his saddle. Pebyn was leaning against the door of a roundhouse leering at him over a mug of ale.

"Hello, Hywel! All alone? No Druid Mabon to protect you? Or Lord Rhys or even clever little Duach to help? Poor Hywel. I do feel so sorry for you." Pebyn was positively purring. "Are you pleased to see me? It's been four years hasn't it since we last met on home ground? Four long years, Hywel, since you had me exiled. Four long years since I've been able ride my own land, eat my mother's cooking and spit in your face. I'm absolutely delighted to see you and I intend to enjoy every minute of our re-union - but you won't!"

Pebyn walked slowly around Mellt, looking up at Hywel with an evil grin. Hywel considered making a bolt for it but the warriors had clustered around closely and one of them grasped Mellt's bridle.

Pebyn turned to the warriors:

"Pull him off is horse and bring him across to me. Four of you get weapons - swords and spears. Keep him covered. I would hate to lose this gift that the Gods have given to me. "

Hywel vaulted off Mellt and used the lull while the warriors went to collect their weapons to send mind messages to his supporters. Firstly, he spoke with Bard Emrys who agreed to send a warband from the llys to rescue him and then he spoke with Duach.

"Just listen, Duach. I've only got a couple of seconds. I've been captured by Pebyn and a dozen Irish warriors in Crosswell. A rescue warband is coming from the llys. But you are much closer so could you bring an armed band of your own men? But don't come up here on your own - Pebyn would like to capture you too. Pebyn's warriors are definitely Irish. You can cut their accents with a knife. I saw their leader with Pebyn at Hwlffordd - he's coming now. I'll have to leave you so that I can concentrate on him."

The Irish leader was a tall, slim, effeminate, young man of about eighteen with curly red hair and a nervous manner. He looked a bit thick but inoffensive enough.

Not at all a natural leader, thought Hywel, and his companions were completely ignoring him. The warrior who exuded natural authority was a big, dark, solemn man in his mid-twenties standing off to one side. Hywel was preparing to monitor his mind when Pebyn started jabbering to the redhead.

"Aidan! This is the pest I've been telling you about - Hywel ap Owain. We were at school together and he got me into all sorts of trouble and a lot of beatings that hurt. He got me thrown out of school by telling lies about me and that's when I came to stay with you in Ireland. I hate him! I hate him! I hate him!" Pebyn's voice grew higher and higher as he spoke and he screamed the last words into Hywel's face.

Aidan looked worried and put a restraining hand on Pebyn's arm.

"Leave him alone, Pebyn. He's a full warrior now, not a schoolboy. And he's in his lord's confidence; remember, he was his shield-bearer at that conference. Hurt Hywel and his lord will take revenge on you."

"He won't," said Pebyn. "I'm under your father's protection and these warriors are my bodyguard. I intend to torture him to pay back the misery he gave me as a child and then, when he has suffered enough, I intend to kill him. ... Watch him grovel!"

Hywel, with an expression of utter boredom on his face, completely ignored Pebyn and looked coolly around the ring of warriors. For all his coolness, Hywel's mind was racing through the minds of the Irish. In general, they were not impressed by Pebyn's outburst and they considered him to be an insignificant insect. The dark, solemn man was sending out strong waves of disgust. Hywel grinned - this should not be too difficult.

Pebyn stepped forward and grabbed a handful of Hywel's tunic.

"Kneel, Hywel ap Owain! Kneel to your master!" he hissed. "When you've grovelled enough I'm going to kill you with horrible tortures!"

Hywel laughed and brushed Pebyn's hand away.

"You and who else, Pebyn?" He waved an arm around the company. "These men are warriors. They might try and kill me in a fair fight, man to man and I wouldn't mind that a bit; I would even enjoy it. But there is no way that they would torture and murder; not for you nor for anyone else. They are warriors - a concept that you don't even begin to understand. You never swore the warrior's oath did you Pebyn? You were too terrified to cope with the training for ten year-olds let alone the warrior tests. You are just an empty bladder of wind."

"B...b...b...but!" protested Pebyn weakly.

Hywel ignored him, turned to the warriors, raised his right hand and quoted solemnly:

"I swear that I will live with honour. ... I swear that I will defend the weak. ... I swear that I will give my life to protect anyone who has sworn this oath."

He smiled at the Irishmen.

"What do you say, gentlemen?"

"WARRIOR!" they shouted back at him in a great roar. "Warrior! Warrior! Warrior!" Then they cheered him and themselves too.

Hywel started to move amongst them as the four with weapons sheathed their swords with much banter. A commanding voice cut through the noise:

"Watch your back!"

Hywel did not hesitate. He dropped to one knee, hunched his back and a body tripped over it. Pebyn fell at his feet with a long knife clutched in his right hand. Hywel sighed in exasperation, rose to his feet, kicked the knife out of Pebyn's hand and stood over him, waiting for him to recover. Pebyn crouched on the ground, blubbering. Finally, Hywel lost patience and dragged Pebyn to his feet.

"Come on, Pebyn! Defend yourself!" he snapped.

"No," muttered Pebyn as he tried to push past Hywel into the safety of the roundhouse.

Hywel hit him a very satisfying blow in the stomach and the watching warriors cheered.

"Do it again, Hywel," shouted an anonymous voice.

"Cathmor!" screamed Pebyn. "Protect me!"

Hywel hit him once more and then kicked him through the door of the roundhouse as the big, dark, solemn man strolled around the group of warriors. Hywel raised his hands in submission and nodded to him.

" He's safe enough from me, sir. It's like punching a jelly. He's too scared to fight back except by stealth or through other people. That's the second time he's seriously tried to kill me. He tried to shoot me from an ambush when we were both ten years old. … And thank you for your warning shout."

"My pleasure. But be careful. Never turn your back on him again. Fight him with weapons and kill him. Challenge him now if you like - I'll make sure it is a fair fight. That way you would make my life easier too," replied the dark man. "My chief has made me his escort - more to keep him out of trouble than to protect him. I can't stand him, or any of his cronies, and I'd like to take my belt to his fat and flabby backside but, for some very strange reason, my chief values him."

"Pebyn's so incompetent with a sword that to fight him would be worse than murder," replied Hywel sadly. "I'd prefer fists but he'll never give me a chance to get at him again. Besides, my chief has forbidden private duels and I'd rather not cross him."

"Never mind," said the dark man; "at least it's given us a chance to meet. I saw you being a very pretty little shield-bearer to your chief at Hwlffordd and I heard you introducing yourself just now. My name is Cathmor and I'm not very pretty but I am a good warrior in all senses of the word." They grinned at each other and shook hands.

"We have a slight problem, sir, and, with your permission I'd like to go and fix it. Our master-at-arms has planned an exercise for today. Two armed warbands are due to rescue me from unspecified perils in this area within the next hour and I'd hate them to think that your warriors are the unspecified peril! They are bound to think that way as soon as they see Pebyn - our enmity is well known. They won't have any warning of your coming either - I'm absolutely certain that Pebyn didn't get permission to bring an armed party into the cantref. But that's his problem and not mine. See you shortly."

As Hywel ran off towards where he knew Mellt was hiding, he sent Duach a frantic mind message.

'Duach! Stop where you are right now. Don't argue! Do it - now!'

'All right, Hywel. I'm stopped. What's the panic?'

'Wheww! No panic. I've flattened Pebyn. All the Irishmen are on my side and they won't obey a word Pebyn says. So, if you come rushing in ready for war you'll cause a nasty incident as well as blowing the secret of my mind skills. I've spread a story saying that

this is a planned rescue exercise for two warbands so play along with it, will you?'

'Of course. Do you want me to leave a couple of men to brief the llys warband as well or do you want me to send them back before they reach you?'

'Warn them and let them keep coming, please. We'll make more plans once you get here. See you soon.'

All this planning on the hoof is tiring thought Hywel as he sent an uncomplicated mind message to Mellt.

"This is Hywel, boy. Come to me. Gently now.' Hywel relaxed as the big black figure emerged from a clump of young trees and cantered towards him. He relaxed too soon - Bard Emrys entered his mind.

'I listened to all that, Hywel. You handled it well. Are you sure that you still want the llys warband to join you?'

'Yes, please. I want to demonstrate that we can't be invaded without a fast reaction from us. Then I want to embarrass Pebyn. The warband will do both nicely. They can escort Pebyn's group home and then mount an obvious guard outside his house until Lord Rhys decides what to do with him. I'll come ahead of them with the senior Irish warrior. He is an exceptionally honourable man and he is wrestling with some decision. I'll find out what's worrying him on our ride back. Got to leave you now. A bewildered Duach has just arrived.'

Hywel brought Duach up to date in a few quick sentences and squashed his desire to kill Pebyn - immediately if not sooner

"No, Duach. He's not important. Leave him to Lord Rhys. The Irishmen despise him and they are all laughing at him. They may well know something about their chief's plans to attack us in the spring and we are more likely to get information out of them if they are friends than if they are enemies. I would like you to take command of both war bands, escort the party to Pebyn's house and make friends with the Irishmen on the way. I've chosen their leader, Cathmor, as my own target and the pair of us will leave for the llys as soon as I can detach him from the others. All right?"

"As you command, lord and master," said Duach, bowing deeply.

"Sorry! I didn't mean to be arrogant! Honest!" replied Hywel. "You can have your revenge later. I'll grovel at your feet and pay penance."

"Get lost, idiot! Go and find your Irishman."

Hywel found his new friend, Cathmor, deep in discussion with Padrick who, not only liked girls, but was also Cathmor's deputy. Both of them were furious and frustrated.

"Hi, Hywel," said Cathmor and sighed deeply. "I've been talking to Pebyn. He refuses to come out of that roundhouse until you have gone. More importantly, he confirms that he didn't get prior permission to bring us here so your warbands are perfectly entitled to attack us on sight. I hope that they don't because I've got no quarrel with them and I don't want to fight them."

"They won't attack you, sir. One band, belonging to my friend Duach arrived a few minutes ago. He is waiting for the other band and will brief them when they come. Then they will all escort you to Pebyn's house."

Cathmor gave a whistle of relief.

"Thanks, Hywel. I owe you."

Then he turned to Padrick.

"Warn our people and get them organised to move. Anyone who acts stupid will answer to me personally. Got it?" Padrick grinned, nodded and left them.

"How well do you know your chief, Hywel?" asked Cathmor diffidently.

"Pretty well. His wife is my grandmother's younger sister. He is a good man, almost as honourable as you, and I respect and trust him beyond all measure."

"Could you take me to see him?"

"Sure. Now?"

"Yes, why not? Pebyn won't move until you've gone - you have damaged his dignity too much - and I no longer want to baby-sit him. He is despicable!"

"He won't want to move when he sees Duach either!" laughed Hywel. "He hates him almost as much as he does me. Shall we go?"

Lord Rhys smiled as Hywel introduced Cathmor and explained how they had met. He stopped Hywel when he started on a tirade against Pebyn.

"Leave it, boy. I will deal with him later. ... It is a pleasure to meet you Cathmor. How can I be of service to you?"

"I'm not sure, sir. My thoughts are a bit confused. Firstly, I would like to apologise for bringing an armed band into your cantref without permission. Only a fortunate meeting with Hywel prevented a fight between us and one of your warbands. I had no idea that Pebyn had not cleared it with you in advance."

Rhys grinned.

"Hywel has his uses. Think nothing of it."

"Secondly, I have been uneasy since we arrived in Wales. The way in which your king has dealt with my chief has not been honourable to you. I had no intention of getting involved in high politics until Hywel recited the warrior's oath at my band to prevent them helping

Pebyn to kill him. He brought me up short. If my own oath meant anything, I needed to talk to you."

"Go on."

"Privately, please, sir?"

"Leave us, Hywel, but follow Druid Mabon's teaching," commanded Lord Rhys.

In other words, monitor his mind, thought Hywel, as he settled himself comfortably on a bench in the corridor.

"Thank you," said Cathmor. He hesitated. "Sir, you said at the conference at Hwlffordd that you were certain that the Irish would attack your cantref in the spring. By the Irish did you mean my chief?"

"Yes."

"You are sure?"

"Certain. I have an excellent network of spies and a very talented team of druids."

"Then you also know that your own king does not like you and will support us against you."

Rhys laughed and nodded.

"Yes. Unless I can terrify him into withdrawing his support but I do not think that doing so is worth the effort. I am not frightened by any attack that your chief can mount but I regret the deaths of brave warriors on both sides that will follow. I would prefer to make an alliance with your tribe so that we can develop the same friendly relationships with you that we have with your neighbours in Wexford. I appreciate that your chief is not in the mood for such a suggestion at the moment but you may put it to him, with my authority, should the situation arise. Would you consider doing so?"

Cathmor looked flabbergasted.

"Me? ... A man you have just met? ... Me? ... You would trust me that far?"

"Have you any reason why I should not?" said Rhys with a grin.

"N... N...no."

"So you will do it then?"

"I would be honoured, lord." said Cathmor, swallowing hard

"Good. I would like to use your time here to show you why I am so confident that no attack against me can succeed. How long are you staying?"

"We are due to meet our ship at the mouth of the Afon Teifi four days from today, sir."

"Right. Hywel can be your escort and guide. Talk to my warriors; look at the terrain; ask anyone, anywhere, whatever you like. I would be happy for you to stay in the llys as my guest but I think that it would be more convenient if you stayed with Hywel."

"Thank you, sir. And my men? There are eleven of them."

"Let Pebyn have the expense of housing them. My son, Pryderi, will organise their entertainment - hunting, perhaps, or races, or warrior competitions, or whatever. He can deal with your deputy. Pebyn will be held under house arrest. I intend to punish him for treason. I'll deal with him tomorrow. ... Let me get Hywel back in. He can take you home and introduce you to his family. Watch his grandmother; she is ferocious!"

Rhys switched rapidly to mind talk.

'Hywel?'

'Yes, lord?'

'Could you get to know this man well enough to monitor his mind and actions when he gets back to Waterford?'

'Yes, lord'

'Do so then.'

Hywel filled Cathmor's next three days with frantic activity. They rode around a lot of the cantref, met and talked with all the most important people and feasted each night with a different family. Cathmor enjoyed most the long talks that he had with Hywel's grandmother. Ferocious she was not. Knowledgeable, politically aware, intelligent and helpful she was. She also helped him to resolve the conflict of loyalties that was tearing him apart.

"You really must not feel guilty about spying on Lord Rhys, Cathmor," she said while they were sitting in her workshop in the garden. The smell of herbs was strong as she crumpled dried thyme for one of her potions. "He wants you to do so. The more you know the better you can present his case to your chief. You have not betrayed your own chief either; Rhys knows that he intends to come and roughly where and when. Your chief cannot bribe people heavily in the next cantref without Rhys hearing about it within days. He does not want to fight but he will if he has to. He has a formidable army and it is brilliantly organised."

And he also has a secret weapon, thought Hywel, grinning to himself in the obscure corner where he sat out of the way. If Rhys' plan worked, he would have a much more effective spy than Cathmor could ever dream of and Rhys would know everything the Irish were planning all the time.

They all jumped as there was a loud bang on the door and Owain appeared.

"Hello, to you all. I thought that you might wish to know that the warning beacon on Dinas Island was lit about half an hour ago and Gwyn's messenger has just arrived. Apparently, a ship has rounded Strumble Head and is aiming in this direction. From Gwyn's description, it is your experimental ship, Cathmor. Do you want to come and watch it? There's no hurry; it will take a couple of hours before we can see it from here but you could climb the hill to get an earlier view."

"It's not worth the effort, thanks," replied Cathmor. "I'll wait."

"I'll come with you, Father," said Hywel. "Can we go out to meet her? Then we could compare her sailing quality with ours." They sat themselves on a bench overlooking the bay.

"No. All our sails are off and the ships are empty and anchored at their winter moorings in the river. Gryffydd is hoping to beach the first one in two days time when the tides are right but I think that we are going to have a problem with the weather. Those clouds mean rain and lots of it. We can't beach if the wind comes too."

"I am so very sorry that I will have started for Gloucester by then and I won't be here to help you," said Hywel solemnly.

"You lying toad," replied Owain amiably. "You know it's a job that you loathe. So you still intend to talk to Aulus then?"

"Yes. This visit by the Irish hasn't changed anything. It is just a distraction and boring too. I know every wrinkle of Cathmor's mind and I will be able to reach him from anywhere. What else has happened since I've been busy?"

"Lord Rhys has declared Pebyn outlaw for bringing an armed band into the cantref and for his second attempt on your life. He is under house arrest until he can be put on board the Irish ship. After that, no one within the kingdom of Dyfed is allowed to help him or to feed him and he can be killed on sight by any warrior.

His lands are forfeit to Rhys who has granted tenure to Edum ap Nislen."

"Whewww!" whistled Hywel. "What did his Irish body-guards think of that?"

Owain laughed.

"They don't know yet. Duach took them out hunting just before dawn yesterday and they planned to camp out overnight. Pryderi collected Pebyn a couple of hours later and took him to the llys under guard. Rhys had assembled the Council and he told us what he intended to do. We agreed. Then we sat in state in the hall while Pebyn stood before us and Rhys pronounced sentence."

"What did Pebyn do?"

"Fell to his knees. Started blubbering. Pleaded with Rhys. Wet himself. Rhys ordered him removed and Edum ap Nislen, with his sword drawn, took him out. ... End of Pebyn."

"I wouldn't mind being the warrior who kills him," growled Hywel.

"Don't boy! You will have to kill men in battle soon enough. It's a horrible job. Your first victim stays with you for ever ... and you will dream about the look in his eyes. Not pleasant dreams. ... Are you ready to leave for Gloucester?"

"Yes. I had planned to leave yesterday so I'll be a maximum of four days late unless I can off-load Cathmor earlier. Iolo has got everything ready to move."

Owain pointed out to sea.

"There's the Irish ship. It's standing well out to sea so it won't be anchoring here. It's definitely making for the Teifi. Go and tell Cathmor."

The Irishman joined them and studied the ship closely.

"How long will it take to get there, Owain?"

"They have timed it badly," he replied. "In this wind they have three to four hours sailing on that course before they can turn towards the estuary. By that time, it will be nearly dark and they would be crazy to do it. They will wait offshore and approach at dawn. The earliest they will be able to take on passengers will be after midday tomorrow. I suggest that you leave here with your party at dawn. That should give you plenty of time."

"So. This is goodbye then. I need to join my warriors tonight so that I can get them organised - and Pebyn too. I would like to thank you both for your friendship and for everything that you have done for me. I regret that the next time that we meet is likely to be at sword-point." He shook his head wordlessly.

Owain punched him lightly on the shoulder.

"Cheer up, man! We won't kill you; we'll just demand a huge ransom that you won't be able to pay. We'll keep you here for ages as our guest and then take you home with honour, and for free. I'd like to see Waterford and all the work that you have been doing to develop new designs of ships. It will be great fun."

"And you don't get rid of me that easily either," added Hywel. "I'll escort you to Pebyn's house when you are ready. We'll talk on the ride. There are some developments that you need to know about Pebyn before you meet him again."

Hywel checked Cathmor's mind when he woke the next morning. All was peaceful at Pebyn's house but not calm. The Irish warriors were in the courtyard, waiting with their horses, and ready to move.

Cathmor was pacing the hall, waiting for Pebyn who was not ready to move; his mother was clinging round his neck like a limpet and shrieking to the gods. Edum ap Nislen was attempting to extradite Pebyn and Lord Pryderi had been called in to help. Hywel grinned and left them to it. He had his own preparations to make.

First, he called Bard Emrys in his mind.

'Good morning, O Great One. I'm making final arrangements to leave at dawn tomorrow. I'd go today but Mellt deserves a rest after rocketing round the countryside with the Irishman. Do you still want to see me before I go?'

'Yes, please, Hywel. Call in as you pass tomorrow. Don't bother to make a special journey today. It's going to pour with rain soon. Those Irishmen are going to get pretty wet - not to mention Pebyn. Such a pity!'

'Me too. I'm going over to Duach to make my peace with him. I'll call in on my way back, mid-afternoon sometime. See you.'

Hywel left him to check on Mellt and Iolo. Mellt was fine but Iolo had developed a tickly cough. Hywel marched him off to his grandmother who produced a small jar of tablets for him to suck on the journey and a potion for him to drink at bedtime.

"That will kill or cure you, boy. Come and see me before you leave in the morning," she commanded. Iolo nodded. "Promise me!" she insisted.

"Yes, lady," stammered Iolo. He was comfortable with all the other members of Hywel's family but his grandmother still terrified him. He scuttled out to fetch one of the family horses for Hywel.

The promised rain started just as Hywel arrived at Duach's house so they took refuge by the big fire in the hall. Duach was over his fury at Hywel leaving him behind on his trip to Gloucester so he could talk sensibly about Hywel's plans.

"I know that you've managed to neutralise Pebyn himself, Hywel, but you were never in any serious danger of a personal attack from him; he would always use someone else to do his dirty work. However, from what Padrick said when we were out hunting, he offered the Irish a huge reward if four of them would stay behind and kill you - they laughed in his face and told him a few home truths. But that doesn't mean that he has stopped trying. He could buy several gangs of bully-boys for half the amount that he offered the Irish - so watch your back."

"That's true," said Hywel, thoughtfully, "but he hasn't had the opportunity to fix it. He's been under house arrest since he came back."

"The guard was on his house to prevent Pebyn leaving, not to prevent other people coming in and out. He's had plenty of opportunity. So I say again, watch your back. And don't forget, they will probably, or even certainly, be strangers to you."

"Thanks, friend. That has really cheered me up!"

"Well, you should let me come with you!"

"Let's not start on that again!" said Hywel, as he got ready to leave. "Look after yourself while I'm away and keep an eye on Bard Emrys for me. I'm off to see him now. Bye."

The bard welcomed him warmly but soon got down to business.

"I was a bit surprised to hear from your grandmother that you are going to Gloucester. Didn't you want to talk it over with me first?"

"No, I didn't. Not because I don't value your advice but because I'm a man now and I need to learn how to make my own decisions - and to live with the results."

"Fair enough. But I'll always be around should you wish to talk and I'd also like you to give me regular reports on your progress. It's better if you call me - I don't want to interrupt something important." The bard paused. "You know that you'll be away during the feast of Samhain?" Hywel nodded. "Well, it's a very dangerous time with all the spirits of the dead wandering freely over the earth and you are more vulnerable than usual as you have only just become a man. You must make absolutely certain that you have taken all the proper precautions to protect yourself and make sure that you are inside a properly protected house."

Hywel looked at him impatiently.

"I know all that! It's beaten into us in childhood!"

"What you don't know, clever clogs, is that those precautions are not foolproof. For that, you need help from your friendly druid." He produced a handful of baked acorns from under his robe and held them out. "Here, these have been specially treated so keep them carefully. Chew one at dusk on the last day of October and then suck one until dawn on the following day. That, and the normal precautions, should keep you safe enough. Have a good journey."

Hywel felt very ashamed of his earlier impatience and smiled at him apologetically.

"I'm sorry, I didn't mean to be rude the other day and I should have realised that you were trying to help me. Thank you. I'll take great care of the acorns but I really must be on my way now. Goodbye."

CHAPTER 9 – AN AMBUSH

It was raining when Hywel and Iolo set out on their journey and it kept raining for days. Hywel kept a sharp look out for archers, ambushes and other signs of hostility but the rain made it very difficult to see anything. They spent the first two nights in comfort with friends who also acted as guides and escorts as far as the gold mines. They talked to the mine guards as they rested the horses and Hywel asked them if any other travellers were moving in the same direction.

"Yes, four men," the biggest guard replied. "They were strange - they didn't want to talk. Said they were in a hurry."

"They were dressed like grooms but they carried swords," said a young, bright looking guard. "I don't think that they were proper warriors. They slouched ... you know ... sort of sloppy."

"Did they say where they were going?" Hywel asked casually. The guards laughed.

" They didn't have to. That track only goes to one place - the pass at Bwlchcefnsarth - and then down to the Tiwy."

"Is there a path down to the Tiwy that doesn't go that way?" Hywel asked.

They shook their heads. "Not within three days ride. Bwlchcefnsarth isn't that far and you should be on the Tiwy well before dusk." Providing we don't get any interference from those four men, thought Hywel.

They reached the famous pass shortly after noon and sheltered in the lee of a huge cluster of rocks to rest the horses and to feed themselves.

"A bit damp, isn't it," said Iolo cheerfully as he tried to stop his bread and cheese from getting soaked before he could eat it.

"Damp! We'd be better off as ducks!"

Hywel didn't like the look of the valley ahead of them one little bit. The path dropped sharply and disappeared round a bend into a thick clump of trees - perfect ambush country. Hywel could see why it had so frightened Cynan and his horses. He wasn't worried about Cynan's monsters but he was worried about a potential ambush.

"Iolo, I've no idea if these men have anything to do with us or not. But since I suspect that Pebyn has paid a gang to kill me, I'm scared of my own shadow. So let's assume that they are going to attack us. We'll go as quietly as we can and, with a bit of luck, we'll surprise them. If they try and stop us, then we charge them as I did at Hwlffordd." Iolo nodded, his eyes alight with excitement. "If we get separated, or if I get hurt, don't stop. Go as fast as you can to a man-mountain, say that you are the son of the grey seal and ask for his help."

"Son of the grey seal," repeated Iolo. "Where do I find him?" Hywel gave him Cynan's instructions then they mounted and set off cautiously down the path.

It was every bit as frightening as Cynan had said. The valley was narrow, steep and twisting. The path was hemmed in by ancient oaks draped in curtains of moss that streamed with water. Mellt stopped suddenly, his ears pricked forward. Hywel listened carefully and could just hear the rumble of voices above the noise of the stream that rushed past on the right. Hywel hesitated then waved to Iolo to dismount. They led the horses back up-stream and tethered them under cover, well off the path.

"There were men talking, Hywel," whispered Iolo. "But I couldn't hear what they were saying."

"Nor could I so let's get closer. We'll leave the horses here."

The valley was very narrow and the trees were too tangled for the boys to move through them silently so they took to the stream. The water was freezing but the high bank of the stream gave them cover and the noise it made masked their slithering sounds. They managed to get really close to the men without being seen. There were only two of them sitting near the stream with a good view of the path and there were four horses tied to trees around a slight bend about twenty metres downstream of them.

Hywel still couldn't hear them very well but one said: "... that big black horse. You can't mistake it."

"I know that," said the one sitting closest to them. "I wish they'd hurry up. I'm soaking. If Pebyn wasn't paying so much, I'd go and find me a nice fire and a girl to warm my bed for me."

"... fool! ... kill. ... Ireland," said the other one.

"Yes, I know he's offered us land in Ireland and we'll need to get away from Wales when we've killed the boy but I don't like the Irish."

Hywel didn't wait to hear any more but moved downstream, out of earshot. Iolo joined him.

"They really do want to kill you!" he whispered indignantly.

Hywel nodded. All his fear and apprehension had vanished and he was seething with fury. Pebyn!!! He really would kill him next time they met. But they needed to get out of this mess first. An idea was struggling out of the back of his mind.

"Iolo. I've got an idea," he whispered. "You are brilliant with horses. Do you think that you could untie those four without disturbing them or being seen by the men?"

"Easy!"

"When you've done that, we'll go back to our own horses and come down the path quietly until they see us. Then we charge them, screaming our war cry as loud as we can. With a bit of luck, we'll get through them, their horses will bolt and they won't be able to follow us. But we'll have to move like lightning once we start our charge. ... Do you think it will work?"

"Yes. But what about the other two men? Where are they?"

"Somewhere up the path, either to give warning or to stop us escaping. I would think that they are probably on the other side of it to the stream, otherwise we would have seen them. ... Shall we try my plan?" Iolo nodded. "Go and fix the horses then."

Iolo was away for ages. Hywel kept sticking his head above the bank but he couldn't see him and everything else was peaceful. Hywel wished that he had gone to fix the horses himself. He had put Iolo in extra danger and he would never forgive himself if Iolo got captured or hurt. He finally came back.

"What kept you?" Hywel hissed.

"The other two men," said Iolo with a grin. "They were pretty close to the horses. I had to move slowly but they didn't see me."

"Thank the gods!"

The plan worked beautifully. They were past the first two men before they could draw their weapons; the horses bolted, knocking over one of the other two and Hywel kicked the last one in the face as he charged past him. Their only problem was avoiding the loose horses, two of which decided to follow them. They eased to a canter and grinned at each other.

"Are all your rides as exciting as this, sir?" asked Iolo innocently.

"Only at the end of September," Hywel replied blandly. "Let's go and find the man-mountain."

He was everything that Cynan had said - huge, happy and hospitable. His small, thin wife smiled at them shyly and produced dry clothing and food with the speed of light. They were both shuddering with cold as they dried themselves and changed. Iolo couldn't stop shuddering even after he had swallowed a huge bowl of steaming broth so their hostess persuaded him to get into bed and, with the help of her eldest daughter, piled so many blankets on top of him that only his eyes and nose were left uncovered. Then she brought a heated stone, wrapped in yet another blanket, and tucked it in by his feet.

"That should warm you up, boy. Try and get some sleep now. ... This is my eldest daughter, Delyth. She will keep you company and wake you in plenty of time for supper."

Delyth hadn't said a word as she had helped her mother to tend Iolo but now she started chattering non-stop. She was a delightful child, about twelve years old, bright and intelligent with the most enchanting, laughing blue eyes. Hywel smiled as she pulled the blankets back from Iolo's face and patted him solicitously; she would be a man-killer when she grew up!

Hywel and the man-mountain settled down to talk.

"Tell me again about these men who were preparing to attack you, Hywel. I've sent one of my men around the village and some of the outlying farms to look for them and to warn my people to keep quiet about you but he won't get far before dark. What did they look like?"

"I didn't see them very clearly, we were moving too fast. They seemed quite ordinary; medium height and build, dressed like grooms, one had a full beard, one was going bald and one will have a black eye after I kicked his face." Hywel grinned. "Some of them may be on foot or they might still be looking for their horses, sir. They bolted with enthusiasm!"

"Yes. That worries me a bit. It was a clever trick but it puts you wrong at law. They could claim that you made an unprovoked attack on them, including kicking one of them in the face. Our lord wouldn't like that very much if they complained to him."

"I don't think that they'll bother the law. They are out to kill me and that's a private fight."

"That worries me too, Hywel."

Hywel looked at him in surprise. Of course it should worry him. It certainly worried Hywel!

He laughed at the boy's expression.

"Yes, that was stupid of me," he rumbled. "I meant that you are very easy to identify by the horse you ride. It's magnificent and everyone here will be talking about it tomorrow. They won't remember you but they will certainly remember your horse. You made a bad mistake by bringing it."

"But I've got an excellent cover story for it."

"Cover stories are only good for the people you tell them to, boy. They won't stop onlookers talking. Leave it here and take one of mine. We can swap them over when you get back. Leave your saddle too. Only rich youngsters can afford saddles. You are supposed to be poor. You might wish to leave your trews off too so that you look like a boy again. Those bandits are looking for a young man. "

"You could be right, sir. Let me think about it overnight. ... As I seem to be ahead of the bandits, I'd like to try and lose them completely tomorrow. That means leaving early and staying away from the main track. Could you possibly lend me someone to show me how to get to Trecastell or even to Aberhonddu by back ways?"

"Of course. And this rain will help to hide you. It will be cold though and you might even get some snow."

Hywel groaned. The rain had been bad enough and he wasn't sure that Iolo could take much more. He hadn't looked at all well. Hywel looked across at the curtained alcove where Delyth sat beside Iolo's bed. He was asleep now with one of his hands held fast in hers. She smiled at Hywel.

Her father noticed his glance.

"I think you've got another problem there, Hywel," he said softly. "That boy was frozen to the marrow. I wouldn't be at all surprised if he comes down with a fever. How important is it that you should leave tomorrow?"

"Time isn't particularly critical although I would like to stay ahead of those bandits. I could wait a day or two but not much longer. If he does have a fever, he won't be able to cope with the rough riding we'll have to do in much under a week. I couldn't wait that long."

Hywel's heart sank. Could he leave Iolo behind and go ahead on his own? He'd have to think hard about that one! What had Cynan said? ... 'The loneliness sears your soul.' Uggh!

Hywel woke before dawn and went to check Iolo who had been restless during the night. He was still fast asleep, breathing loudly through his mouth. His skin felt damp and sweaty as Hywel touched it so he didn't have a fever - yet. It would have been dry and burning hot if he had. He sent a prayer to the god of medicine - 'Please let it be only a cold. Please.'

The man-mountain stirred under his blankets and yawned noisily as Hywel went out to check the weather. It was just his luck! The sun's rays were streaking upwards from behind the big mountains into a clear, powder blue sky with not a single cloud in sight. Hywel couldn't see the big mountains themselves because the foothills hid them but even the foothills would be a severe challenge and he was eager to get started. But he couldn't get started yet - there was Iolo.

A brisk, middle-aged man came into the fenced enclosure that surrounded the house and introduced himself to Hywel as the man-mountain's steward. He explained that two strangers matching his description had spent the night in the village and one of them wanted to buy a horse.

"He has the biggest black eye you've ever seen," said the steward with a grin. "I've just left him. He isn't breathing or talking too well either. I reckon you've broken his nose. ... Let's go and tell Hafgan."

Hafgan was making severe inroads into a haunch of venison as they went back into his house. He waved them towards a loaded table while Delyth brought them ale.

"What news?" he asked his steward thickly. The man explained and Hafgan turned to Hywel. "What do you want to do, Hywel? We can hold them up a bit for you by having trouble finding a suitable horse but the other two will be ahead of you by now."

Hywel nodded.

"I've got an idea, sir. But I'll need your help." He explained what he wanted him to do. Hafgan spluttered with laughter and agreed.

The steward brought up a sturdy two-wheeled cart pulled by a pair of ponies and they helped Hafgan to climb in.

"Like it, Hywel?" he asked as he settled himself comfortably.

"Yes sir. Very smart."

"I had it built when I could no longer find a horse strong enough to carry me. This works fine and it can go pretty fast on flat ground. Stopping it then is not so easy but I think I've got the hang of it now."

The steward led them to the roundhouse where the strangers had spent the night. Hywel went in first and glared at the two men without speaking as he checked their minds. As he had hoped, the one with the broken nose had been Pebyn's personal groom while he was at school with him. Hafgan struggled through the door and sat on a bench, which groaned under his weight. He sat silent and glowered - hugely impressive.

"Stand up to greet the lord of this land," Hywel snapped at the two men who looked totally bewildered.

"What are your names?" growled Hafgan. They told him. He pointed to the one with the broken nose. "What are you doing on my land?"

"N... nothing, lord," stammered the man, "We were just passing through."

"From where to where?"

"From Cemais to Aberhonddu, lord."

"Why?"

"I ..."

"Our chief sent us, lord," broke in the second man.

"I didn't ask you," said Hafgan. "Keep your mouth shut." The man deflated.

"I asked you, broken-nose. Why are you travelling from Cemais to Aberhonddu? And why do you want to buy a horse? And who is your chief."

"Our chief is Pebyn ap Cynan ap Teynon, lord."

By this time the two men were completely demoralised and it was time for Hywel to join in.

"These are the men we've been warned about, lord, but there should be four of them." He turned to broken-nose. "Where are the others?"

"They went on ahead and they'll wait for us in Aberhonddu, sir."

"You are wanted by High Druid Mabon of Cemais for questioning about an attempted murder four years ago. He has asked all chiefs to close their borders to you and your companions," Hywel said and nodded to Hafgan.

"I will not have you on my land," said Hafgan sternly. "Nor will I let anyone aid you or sell you a horse. My men will escort you and your companion to the gold mines at Dolaucothi where they will hand you over to the guards there. They will look after your weapons on the way. ... Outside, both of you."

"But, lord!" protested broken-nose.

Hafgan stood up and towered menacingly over his slight figure. "Outside I said. GO!"

The men fled without waiting to collect their belongings.

Hywel went to the door and watched Hafgan's men usher the two bandits away. Then he turned back into the room. Every ounce of Hafgan was quivering with silent laughter. He grinned at the sight and let him out of his misery.

"They've gone, sir. You can make a noise now."

His bellows of laughter shook the walls and tears ran down his huge cheeks.

"Oh, Hywel!" he spluttered. "If only they knew! That's the best bluff I've ever seen. You'll go far, boy. Two enemies neutralised by a baby spy and a village headman without a single blow. Beautiful!"

Hywel was equally cheerful.

"With a bit of luck, sir, the warriors at Dolaucothi will hold them until they get orders from their own chief. It wouldn't surprise me if they got passed all the way back to Cemais under escort. I'd love to see Druid Mabon's face when they arrive!"

It was time he spoke to Bard Emrys in his mind and he'd warn him that they might be coming. He would do it when he'd checked on Iolo.

Hafgan was still talking: ".... bought you at least two days grace. When are you going to leave?"

"That depends on Iolo, sir. Can I go and check on him?"

"Help me into my cart, then."

They returned slowly to his house to find a miserable Iolo sitting up in bed with Delyth in close attendance.

"Hello, sir," he said thickly. "I god a coud in by dose ad I can'd stad up."

Hywel laughed at him.

"Poor Iolo. Stay there until you feel better. Keep yourself warm."

He went to find his hostess.

"It's really pulled him down, Hywel," she said. "He was too weak to stand this morning and even if it doesn't go down onto his chest, which it probably will, he really shouldn't travel for at least a week and even then only slowly and in good weather. You'd best leave him behind and collect him on your way back. I'd be very happy to look after him ... and so would Delyth," she added with a smile.

Hywel went and sat outside in the sunshine feeling absolutely miserable. He couldn't risk Iolo's health by taking him with him in his present state and he couldn't kick his heels here until he was fit enough to cope with the journey ahead. He would have to leave Iolo behind and go on by himself. What made it worse was that he would have to leave Mellt as well. It was quite clear that the remaining bandits could only recognise him by his horse and he would be stupid to take him, particularly if the bandits warned the Silures that he was a spy. Pebyn certainly knew that he was a spy - he had blabbed it around at Hwlffordd - and he was likely to have told his men. Uggh! Maybe it was all getting too difficult and he should turn back? And face his father? And Lord Rhys? And Duach? And what about Aulus? Hywel laughed. He would leave on his own - for Gloucester.

The decision taken, Hywel went to fix the details. The worst part was telling Iolo who burst into tears and stammered his objections as well as he could through his blocked nose and sore throat. Hywel consoled him slightly by making him totally responsible for Mellt. In turn, Iolo promised that he would not ride out without an escort just in case the bandits returned and mistook him for Hywel.

CHAPTER 10 – A LONELY JOURNEY

It was still well before noon, the weather was good and Hywel reckoned that, given Cynan's directions, he could get to Trecastell or even to Aberhonddu by nightfall if he started now. There was no point in using anything other than the direct route as the two bandits up ahead would not recognise him without Mellt and Iolo particularly if he left his saddle and saddlebags behind. That would certainly make him look poorer and more unimportant.

He packed the bare essentials in a leather bag he borrowed from his host - flint, iron and kindling to make a fire, a small iron pot, food, his flute, his Roman token and a spare tunic. There was no need to carry water; the gods would provide plenty of that from the sky! He slung the bag over his shoulder, climbed onto Iolo's horse, waved goodbye to the man-mountain and his family, took a deep breath and left on his journey into the unknown.

The view back over the broad valley of the Tywi was fantastic and the few scudding clouds threw shadows that made the landscape itself appear to move. Hywel climbed steadily through a forest for most of the day and followed the small cairns marking the route very carefully. The forest was too thick for him to see any distance and the cairns and the noise of the stream were his only guides.

Hywel saw only one house during the climb - a small, neat roundhouse set in a tiny fenced enclosure near the stream. A small, wiry man and a young boy were tending to one of three charcoal stacks set downwind of the house.

"Good day to you," said the man cheerfully. "Why don't you rest your horse and come in and tell us your news. We don't get many travellers at this time of year."

"Thank you," Hywel replied as he dismounted. "I'm on my way to Trecastell. Is it far?"

"Not very. About three kilometres. You'll be there well before dark. Come in."

Hywel tied his horse to the fence and followed him inside.

"Are you hungry?" Hywel hesitated, the smell of the hare stew in the pot was tantalising but these people were obviously pretty poor. "There's plenty," encouraged the man.

Hywel smiled.

"No, thank you. I've been staying down with Hafgan and he's filled me so full of food that I can hardly move. It will be several days before I feel hungry again."

The man laughed.

"How is the old monster? He's due to send someone up for charcoal before the snows start."

"He's fine and as large as ever. He was sorting out two suspicious characters when I left. He thought that they were bandits and sent them back over the border to Dolaucothi. They said they had two friends who may have come this way. Have you seen them?"

His wife handed Hywel a mug of ale as her husband scowled and drank deeply.

"Yes," he growled. "An ill mannered pair. They rode past without even answering my greeting."

"When?"

"Late yesterday. It was raining and they had their hoods pulled well down. They were in a hurry too. But they could have said 'Hello'. ... Louts!"

"So you didn't see them clearly?"

"No. One of them was riding a piebald though. The other had a dark roan with a white hind foot. And I think that they were carrying swords."

They were obviously the missing pair but how right Hafgan had been to stop him riding Mellt, thought Hywel. In this part of the world horses were easier to recognise than people. He chatted to the man for a while about inconsequential things and then took his leave.

Hywel spent the night at Trecastell where there was no sign of the bandits. The next morning he rode towards Aberhonddu very slowly as he tried to work out how best to tackle his two enemies while still preserving his cover amongst the locals. No ideas came at all.

He was feeling very odd - a combination of tense, lonely and bored. He missed Iolo badly and it would have helped enormously to have been able to discuss decisions before making them. He felt himself getting more and more wound up and wary as he approached Aberhonddu.

He paused on a ridge overlooking the village and studied it carefully. The fort sat on a bluff off to one side and overlooked the village that was big, much bigger than Nanhyfer, and set well back from the three rivers that converged upon it. Its hundred or so round-houses were spread between the river Gwys and the east bank of a smaller, fast flowing river that joined the Gwys from the north. A big, evil-looking river came in from the south, right across his path, and joined the Gwys about half a kilometre upstream of the village. All three rivers were in spate but, fortunately, had not yet broken their banks. Once they did, they would form an impenetrable lake that would block the route Hywel was using. That was something to remember for his return journey - if he ever made it! He shook himself to get rid of his depression and rode forward.

The track ahead of him crossed a rickety bridge over the southern river and carried on to second bridge that led into the village. A boy of around twelve was sitting near the second bridge, idly throwing stones into the river. He looked up and smiled as Hywel dismounted and led his horse cautiously over the bridge.

"Phew! I'm glad that's over," he said as he sat down beside the boy.

"Have you come far?" he asked.

"From Trecastell. I'm supposed to be meeting my uncle here tomorrow. If he doesn't come, I've got to go on to Bwlch. ... It's a bit cold to be playing with stones, isn't it?" Hywel said as the boy lobbed another into the river.

He laughed and rolled onto his back.

"I don't mind. A man is paying me to do it."

"Paying you? You must be joking!"

"No, honest! He's staying at my father's inn and he wants me to look for a big black horse. He say's it's magnificent and that I can't miss it. It hasn't come yet."

"And the rider?"

"He didn't know anything about him - just that he was a young man and that he would have a groom with him."

"What's the man look like?"

"Just a man," shrugged the boy. "He's got a piebald horse."

Hywel thought for a moment. He had to stay somewhere and he would like to check these men's minds to see what they were planning next. They didn't know what he looked like so it was worth the risk.

"Do you think that your father would have room for me to stay while I wait for my uncle?" he asked the boy.

"Well ... he doesn't normally take boys. Can you pay?"

"Yes, if he doesn't charge too much," laughed Hywel. "But I've got a better idea. I'm an apprentice bard and I could play my flute for my supper."

"That sounds smashing. There's no one in sight and I'm hungry. I'll take you home. Come on." He got to his feet and started leading Hywel into the village.

"My name's Ifor. What's yours?" he said over his shoulder.

Hywel was glad Ifor couldn't see the surprise on his face. He hadn't thought about it but he couldn't use his own name because the two men would know it. He had better become his youngest uncle.

"I'm Madog ap Meredith," he replied.

Ifor's father was a tall, lean man with long moustaches. He was suspicious and unhelpful.

"Why are you travelling alone? You're only a boy. I don't like boys here. Inns are only for men," he growled.

"I'm an apprentice bard, sir. My voice has just broken and my master's sent me back to my family for a bit. My father died last year and my mother has gone to live with her brother. He lives near Bwlch but I don't know where. He said that he'd try to met me here."

"Can you pay?"

"Yes, sir. I have a little money."

"All right. Ifor will look after you. Keep out of the way of the other guests."

They haggled over the price for a bit and Hywel paid him from the few coins that he kept in the purse hanging from his belt. He kept his silver and gold coins well hidden - sewn into the seams of his tunic and cloak.

Ifor went back to his bridge and Hywel wandered round the village. Although Lord Rhys didn't need the information, he thought that it would be good practice for him to assess the defences, the approaches and the people of this place. The people were easy. Mostly they were pleasant and cheerful and they lived the same sort of lives as the people did in Nanhyfer. There was a smith, a potter, a carpenter and a small market place that was empty at the moment as the market was held only once a week in winter. He climbed up to the fort that was in pretty good repair. The warrior on guard at the main gate was very relaxed - sitting on a bench and chatting to a girl. Lord Rhys would have a seizure if that happened at Nanhyfer!

Suddenly Hywel was hit with a wave of homesickness. He longed for familiar routines and rituals. He wanted to hug his grandmother. He wanted to hear his uncle Tegwyn's laugh and his father's quick rejoinder. He wanted to be sailing on a limitless sea with Gryffydd's strong arm around his shoulder as he steered the ship. Instead, he sat on a rock, staring blindly to the north, until he mastered his scalding tears.

He spoke to himself severely. 'Cynan warned you. You knew it was going to be like this. You could have waited until Iolo was well. It is your own choice. You told your father that you were a man now and had to make your own decisions and live with the consequences. These are the consequences - face up to them!' ... He sat on his rock for a long time.

The inn was full when he returned to it shortly before dusk. He found Ifor in the next roundhouse that the family used as a kitchen for the inn, a store and their own sleeping quarters. He was loading a tray with spoons and pottery bowls to take next door while his mother stirred a large cauldron of stew. He greeted Hywel cheerfully and introduced him to his mother who smiled and nodded.

"Hey, Madog. Could you give me a hand? We're run off our feet tonight," he said.

"Of course," Hywel replied. The two bandits would never suspect him if he appeared to be one of the family.

"What would you like me to do?"

"Grab that basket of bread and the ladle and follow me." They went through to the other roundhouse and put their burdens on the central table. "Now come and help me with the cauldron." It was heavy and difficult to carry as it swung between them. It was also hot and Hywel yelped as it brushed against his leg. Ifor grinned. They put it on the floor next to the table with the bread on it.

"I'll put the stew into the bowls," said Ifor, "and you carry it to the men while my father collects their money. All right?" Hywel nodded and set about his task.

He quite enjoyed his stint as an inn servant. The guests were all relaxed and happy and they completely ignored him as he scurried round with stew, bread and mugs of ale. He had plenty of time to monitor the minds of his two targets and they weren't terribly informative.

They were not surprised that they hadn't found him today and they were prepared to wait for a week. If he hadn't appeared by then he had obviously escaped and they might as well give up and go home. A pity about Pebyn's money but that was life. At least they wouldn't have to go to Ireland if Hywel didn't turn up. They were worried about the two companions that they had left behind. They should have been here today but there was no point in going back to look for them. They would either come tomorrow or not at all. The reward would be divided between all four of them even if only two took part in the killing. They were happy men.

Hywel grinned inside himself at several of their conclusions and went back to the kitchen with Ifor for his own meal. It was extremely good as his mother had made special dumplings to go with the family's stew and they were delicious. She then showed Hywel to a pallet that she had put alongside Ifor's bed and he snuggled down for the night.

He was just dropping off to sleep when Bard Emrys came into his mind.

'Hi, Hywel! How's the solo-spy?'

'Fine, thanks. Comfortably settled in an inn at Aberhonddu.'

'Tell me about your trip.'

Hywel ran quickly through what had happened, leaving out his internal conversations when sitting on the rock.

'So you're on your own now. Do you want us to send a party to rescue Iolo and Mellt?'

'No, thanks. There's no point. They are safe and comfortable and the man-mountain is quite happy to house them. I'll pick them up on the way back.'

'All right. But I think that I'll go and talk with Pebyn's mother for you. It's time we stopped this nonsense.'

'We still haven't got any real proof.'

'No. But if I tell her that Mabon is protecting you from the Otherworld - which is why I know about it - then she should be too frightened to start anything else.'

'Maybe. It's certainly worth a try. But I reckon that the only way to stop it is for me to kill Pebyn.'

They talked about inconsequential things for a while before he left Hywel, remarkably comforted. He had forgotten his mind-skills during his homesickness. He wasn't really on his own. He could always talk to Emrys.

Hywel had a carefree ride to Bwlch the next day and he found Cynan's friend, Idwal, without difficulty. He welcomed Hywel to his llys and offered him hospitality for the night. They talked about Cynan for a while and then Hywel disclosed himself.

"Sir, Cynan also sends you greetings from the Grey Seal. I am his son," he said quietly.

Idwal looked at him with a raised eyebrow.

"Are you, indeed!" he said, equally quietly. "A bit young for it, aren't you?" Hywel just grinned.

"Come with me. It's too public to talk here."

He led Hywel to his private apartments and sent his servant for wine. "Right. Tell me a bit about yourself. I know that Cynan had no children so you must be a professional relation."

"My non-professional name is Hywel ap Owain and my father is a trader and a shipmaster. I sailed with him, met and became friends with some Romans in Gloucester. My chief has been asked to provide warriors to support the king of Gwent in an attack against them in the spring. He wants to know more about the local situation before he will commit himself and he has sent me to find out. It is my first trip and Cynan reckoned that I could use some help. He thought that you might be prepared to provide it."

Idwal smiled.

"I might but, on the other hand, I might not. You've told me a lot more than you should have done. I could have you killed. Why did you trust me?"

"Cynan trusted you with his life, sir. I could do no less."

"All right, young Hywel. What do you want to know?"

Hywel felt dizzy with relief and grinned at him weakly.

"Just about everything, please, sir, but mostly, what are the men of Gwent like? What sort of leaders do they have? Would they make trustworthy allies? How many warriors do they have? Have they the resources to feed large numbers of allies as well as their own men? Things like that."

Idwal started to talk. He gave Hywel all the information he needed and a lot more. They talked until the supper horn sounded when he stretched and grinned.

"I'm afraid that, to keep your cover, Hywel, I'm going to have to ignore you for the rest of your stay. I wish you well on your mission and my llys is always open to you. Take care, baby seal, and don't be so trusting - it will get you killed. Goodbye."

Hywel bowed.

"Thank you, sir. I am exceedingly grateful for everything that you have done for me. I'll be a great big, tough, bull seal by the time you see me next. Goodbye."

Hywel spoke to Bard Emrys in his mind that night and passed on everything that Idwal had told him. Idwal had warned him of a huge, vicious, sadistic warrior called the Bear who lived in Y Fenni. Apparently, he enjoyed torturing and killing people - any people. He had crippled and killed several of his own men in mock combat but he was equally happy to torture casual passers by. Hywel thought that it was important to get his information home, just in case he met this monster and couldn't go any further.

CHAPTER 11 – THE BEAR

Hywel felt that he needed to confirm at least a part of Idwal's information with his own eyes so he planned to stop the next night in Y Fenni. He wanted to arrive there towards dusk so he started out late the next morning and rode slowly along the flat, wide bottom of the Gwys valley. The people he met looked much the same as those he had met earlier and they were doing the same sort of things but they didn't laugh as much and they had a closed-in sort of expression on their faces. They were perfectly polite if Hywel spoke to them but they didn't start any conversations. It was weird. Nobody took any notice of him unless he spoke - he could have been an invisible ghost and this made him very uneasy. He was dead scared at the thought of spending the night in the middle of a suspicious and potentially hostile village, particularly as it housed the Bear.

The few people around stared at him as he rode through the outskirts of the big village just before dusk and into its central space. He stopped and slid off his horse to talk to a villager who directed him to a roundhouse that he said was an inn. The innkeeper was as uncooperative as Ifor's father had been but he grudgingly agreed that Hywel could spend the night there. He was just starting on his supper when a warrior came and stood in front of him. Hywel got to his feet and smiled at him. He was fully armed, including a spear, and he looked at Hywel coldly.

"Who are you, boy, and what are you doing here?" His voice was deep and gruff.

"My name is Hywel, sir. I am an apprentice bard but my voice hasn't yet settled down after breaking and my master has given me permission to visit my grandfather who lives in Lydney. I am resting here for the night."

Shut up! Hywel told himself fiercely. The more you talk, the more you give away. Just answer his questions and look humble.

"What is your master's name?"

"Bard Emrys, sir," Hywel said as shyly as he could manage.

"What instruments do you play?"

"The flute, sir."

"Fetch it and come with me."

He led Hywel to a large rectangular hall made of wood where two warriors were standing guard outside the door and many more were eating inside. A third, big, burly warrior, even bigger than Tegwyn, stood to one side holding a riding whip between his hands. Hywel's heart sank. Was this the Bear? There was a twisted grin on his dark face as he told Hywel's escort to stop.

"What have we here?" the big man asked the escort.

"The innkeeper sent for me, sir. This boy is travelling on his own. He claims to be an apprentice bard going to see his grandfather at Lydney. The innkeeper thought that he might be a spy and sent for us."

"Did he indeed. Bring him over here."

The big man moved towards a shed that was lit with two large flares on its outside walls. Hywel's escort pushed him and he stumbled after what had to be the Bear.

"Your name, boy?" the big man demanded.

"Hywel ap Owain, lord."

"Strip, Hywel ap Owain," he commanded.

Hywel stared at him in amazement. Then his escort's spear hit him viciously, full across his back, and he fell flat on his face. He couldn't breathe! And his back felt as though it was broken! A hand grabbed his hair, hauled him to his feet and dangled him so that his toes just touched the ground. It was agony and his eyes watered as he gasped for breath.

"Crying already," jeered the big man. "I haven't even started yet." He shook Hywel as a dog shakes a rat.

Hywel screamed. He just couldn't stop himself; the pain was so bad. Then the man dropped him and he collapsed on the ground.

"I told you to strip, boy. I want to check your tribal marks. You have until I count to ten." He slashed his riding whip across Hywel's shoulders. "One ..."

Despite his agony, Hywel started to tear his clothes off as fast as he could then stood in front of the man, naked and shivering with a mixture of cold and terror, by the time he reached a count of nine.

"Much better, little man," purred his tormentor as he walked round Hywel, examining him closely, touching and handling him as he would a horse. He kicked his feet apart and Hywel's skin crawled as the man's hands reached his private parts.

"Bit small aren't you, boy?"

Hywel stood rigid and silent. The man's huge, hard fingers tightened and twisted.

"Answer me!"

Hywel groaned in agony.

"As you say, lord," he panted through his pain and humiliation.

His knees gave way and he slid through the man's hands to huddle on the ground.

"Oh, no, worm," said the hateful voice. "I haven't finished yet. Stand up." The whip slashed across Hywel's buttocks. "I said stand up."

Another slash. Every muscle that Hywel had was quivering in pain as he forced himself to his feet and he could not stop the tears that were pouring down his face. He hung his head, trying to regain his courage while he waited for the next onslaught.

"Why do you bear the mark of the druid?" the man demanded as poked the blue line on Hywel's chest.

Hywel took an involuntary half a step backwards and was held in position by his escort's spear.

As quick as a flash the leather loop at the end of the whip flicked in between his legs and Hywel screamed in agony.

"Stand still!" roared the big man. "And answer my question or I'll do that again but harder!"

"B... b... because I'm going to be a bard, lord."

"That is the mark of a warrior, not a bard. Are you a warrior, worm?"

"I'm an apprentice bard, lord."

The whip threatened again and Hywel flinched in anticipation.

"Not good enough. Are you a warrior?"

Then the big man's attention switched away from Hywel to a warrior approaching him from the hall.

"The chief wants you urgently, sir," panted the newcomer. "He's in the hall."

The big man started to move then looked over his shoulder to Hywel's escort.

"Get him dressed and bring him to me in the hall."

Hywel gave a huge sigh of relief and he collapsed to the ground.

"Yes, sir," replied the escort.

Hywel groaned as the spear thumped into his back, making the earlier blows all burn like fire.

"Listen and listen good, boy," he hissed as Hywel lay in front of him. "That was the Bear and he can do no wrong in the eyes of our chief. If you want to live, do exactly as he says. No more and no less. Understand?" Hywel nodded.

"And tell him what he wants to know or he will kill you. Understand?"

"Yes, sir," said Hywel weakly.

"Get dressed then, as quick as you can."

This was very difficult as Hywel's head was a thumping drum of pain, he couldn't breathe properly, his back and legs were agony and his arms didn't work too well. He managed it eventually and stood hunched and swaying in front of his escort.

"Walk!" he snapped.

Hywel couldn't. He took one pace and fell to his knees. The escort poked him with his spear.

"Walk!" he commanded.

Hywel collapsed into a crumpled heap. All his muscles had locked solid. His escort swore and heaved him to his feet by his clothes and called to the guards for help. Two of them half carried Hywel into the hall and dropped him on his knees in front of a small, dark man with beady, intelligent eyes who was sitting in the centre of the top table with the Bear at his right hand.

"I was questioning this worm when you called me, lord," said the Bear. "He says that his name is Hywel and that he's an apprentice bard. You might like to check that out. If he's a bad musician, he's more than likely a spy and I'll question him again."

Hywel gulped and prayed to the god of the bards.

"It looks as though you've half killed him already," said the chief. "Give him water, somebody."

A mug was thrust into Hywel's hands and he drank gratefully.

"What's your name, boy?"

Hywel coughed to clear his throat and his chest hurt.

"Hywel ap Owain, lord," he managed to whisper.

"Are you really a bard?"

He shook his head, which was a mistake as a shaft of pain nearly blinded him.

"An apprentice bard, lord."

"Then play me something to prove it."

The escort handed Hywel his flute which had survived undamaged and, still on his knees, he started to play a song of victory. It was the hardest thing that he had ever done. He hurt so much he wanted to die but he managed to produce bright, cheerful music.

The warriors sitting around the tables were soon singing loudly and enthusiastically. They banged their beakers on the table as he finished, and called for more. The chief nodded and Hywel managed to play a second tune.

"All right, apprentice bard, you've proved your point," said the chief. "Now, tell me where you are going next - if I agree."

"I want to go to Lydney, lord, to visit my grandfather. I've been told to cross the Wye at Trefynwy and to ask for directions from there."

The chief turned to the Bear.

"What do you think?"

He shrugged.

"He's harmless enough but I'd like to question him a bit more. Keep him here under guard tonight and then send him under escort to Raglan when I've finished with him."

"I don't like strangers wandering round here, boy," said the chief, "nor does my king who lives in the llys at Ysgyryd Fach. I'll provide you with an escort part of the way to Trefynwy. Don't ever enter our lands again without my personal permission."

Hywel was still on his knees but he bowed as well as he could. His escort dragged him to his feet. This time his legs worked after a fashion and he staggered outside. The escort took him across to the hut where the Bear had questioned him, lifted the bar across the door and motioned him inside.

Hywel hesitated on the threshold and turned to face his escort.

"Sir … ?" he asked timidly.

"Yes."

"Could I have some water, please? I'm terribly thirsty."

"No," said the escort as he rammed the butt of his spear into Hywel's stomach and sent him flying backwards into the far wall of the hut. Hywel heard the door slam and the locking bar drop into place as he buried his head in his arms and burst into tears.

Hywel had recovered some of his courage by the time that a young warrior collected him the following morning. He still hurt badly and in places that he had never hurt before. His injuries had stiffened and he could hardly move. He was also hungry and horribly thirsty but the warrior hadn't brought any water, just Hywel's horse, his cloak, his flute and his leather bag.

"Come out, boy. Let's get moving."

He seemed nervous and edgy as he helped Hywel onto his horse and started to move towards the gate.

"STOP!"

Hywel's heart sank. It was the Bear. He sauntered across to them.

"So! A baby leading a worm."

The warrior sat rigidly at attention; his eyes fixed on the tree in front of him. Hywel started trembling as the Bear walked around him repeating his tactics of the previous night. He stood behind Hywel for what seemed ages.

"Down! Both of you," he snapped.

They dismounted and stood submissively in front of him.

"I want this worm bound and blindfolded until you are past the king's llys at Ysgyrd Fach," the Bear told the young warrior. "You can take his blindfold off then but keep his hands and feet tied until you reach Raglan. Go and get rope. Understand?"

"Yes, sir," replied the warrior. He saluted smartly then went off on his errand.

The Bear grinned at Hywel and licked his lips.

"Frightened, are you, worm?"

"Yes, lord."

"Hurt, are you, worm?"

"Yes, lord."

"Warrior, are you, worm?

"No, lord."

"Spy, are you, worm?"

"No, lord."

The Bear was behind Hywel again and he nearly panicked but forced himself to stand still. The Bear poked Hywel hard in the ribs and he gasped in pain.

"Let's try that again. On your knees, worm."

Hywel dropped. Then the Bear put his foot flat against Hywel's back and pushed him forward onto his face.

"That's a good position for a worm. Stay there."

Hywel bit his cloak to stop the sobs of terror that were building up in his throat and then he heard footsteps.

"What have you got there, Bear?" asked the chief.

"Only last night's worm."

"Leave it. I want to go and inspect our defences around Bwlch. I'm not satisfied that we've got our lookout points in the right places. The escort is bringing our horses now."

"I thought that we were going tomorrow? I intended to play with my worm today."

"Leave it. It is too battered to give you much entertainment. You can find another victim. Besides, bards are chancy people. They can summon up spirits from the Otherworld. It is better not to get involved with them."

The Bear laughed incredulously.

"This worm?" He kicked Hywel. "This worm summon spirits? You must be joking!"

"He could have a powerful protector. Anyway, I had a bad dream about him last night. Let him go."

"All right. He wasn't providing much sport anyway." The Bear kicked Hywel again; this time hard in the thigh.

"You're lucky again, worm. Stay there until your warrior comes back."

Hywel's young warrior had the sense to stay hidden until the Bear, his chief and their escort had clattered away.

Hywel raised his head and saw him approaching. He knelt beside Hywel.

"Are you all right?" he asked anxiously.

"Only two kicks but they were worse than kicks from a horse. ... " Hywel groaned. "I hurt all over and I'm not sure which bit hurts most."

"You've been lucky. Last week in weapon practice he broke my friend's arm and then hit him on the head so hard he's still unconscious. I hate him but I'm also terrified of him. ... I'm going to have to blindfold you and tie you up like he said. Somebody is sure to tell him if I don't and then he'll kill me. But I've brought you a flask of water. Have a drink before we start."

Hywel took the first mouthful, and used his tongue to rub it round his teeth before spitting it onto the ground. Then he drained the flask slowly.

"Thank you, my friend. May the gods smile on you for ever," he said as he handed the flask back.

He then sat on a bench while his escort wound a cloth around his eyes.

"There, that looks good," he said when he finished. "But you should be able to see under the bottom of it. Can you?"

Hywel twisted and turned his head. He could see quite clearly if he tilted his head back.

"Yes, that's great. Thanks."

"Now for your hands." He tied them firmly but not painfully. "Mount now, before I fix your feet."

Hywel climbed onto the bench and from there onto his horse. The pain was agonising as he sat on the horse - and he could not stop his groans – they would have been screams if he had been on his own.

Then the warrior tied Hywel's right ankle, took the rope under the horse's belly and tied the left. Hywel could move his legs a bit but not enough to use his knees and thighs to raise himself off the horse's back. He gritted his teeth in anticipation. This was going to hurt - badly.

"I'll loosen that once we get past Ysgyrd Fach," the warrior whispered, "but it's got to look good enough to get us out of here." He mounted. "Ready?"

Hywel laughed. Ready to leave this place?

"Ready, waiting, desperate - take your pick!"

His spirits were soaring and he felt as free as a bird, despite his bonds and the pain to come.

The warrior led him gently and slowly down through the village and onto the track that ran alongside the river. Hywel was unbalanced and awkward and he couldn't see well enough to anticipate the horse's movements so he hurt - very badly indeed. By the time they got to a hidden clearing on the far side of Ysgyrd Fach and stopped his thighs and private parts were bruised, squashed, rubbed raw and burned like fire.

His escort untied his hands and feet first then helped him to the ground. Hywel lay flat on his back, which hurt so much he nearly screamed, stretched out his legs and groaned as his escort took off the blindfold.

"Here, have another drink," he said, offering a small wineskin. It tasted like the nectar of the gods. "The Bear makes us all do a five kilometre cross-country gallop with our legs tied like that when we join the warband - and he rides with us. I screamed with pain every time I jumped a hedge and there were a lot of hedges. ... He likes to hear people scream."

"He's possessed by evil spirits and he should be killed like a mad dog," Hywel said with absolute conviction.

"Nobody's strong enough to kill him," the escort said mournfully. "Don't think that we haven't thought about it, often."

"An arrow then or poison."

The warrior shook his head.

"Tried it. Didn't work. He crippled his escort commander when someone shot an arrow at him. The poison made him sick but didn't kill him. He beat the cook to death with his own hands."

"Uggh! I'm glad that he's your problem and not mine."

Hywel levered himself painfully to his feet and staggered towards the stream where he buried his face in the water. It was bliss. His head stopped aching and he absorbed the liquid like a drooping plant. Then he stripped off his clothes and lay immersed in the freezing water until the pain in his various cuts and bruises was deadened and the water had washed him clean, both physically and mentally. He began to feel half-human after he fished the clean tunic out of his bag and finished dressing. His companion completed the job.

"Have some food," he said, offering his rations.

"Thank you." Even the marching rations tasted good.

"They didn't disturb my pack so I've got some apples, cheese and stale bread if you'd like some," Hywel said thickly. They shared their supplies and gorged themselves full.

"I've been thinking," said the warrior as they finished. "We need to be on our way soon and we need to make it look as though you are still trussed up." Hywel groaned. "I know, but I'm not prepared to be killed by the Bear, even for you. ... So, how about we wind rope around your wrists and ankles as though you were bound. Then we tie a loose rope right around your horse's belly. If we meet anyone, you slide your feet inside the rope and also hold your hands together. That way you'll look as though you're tied up. Otherwise you just ride normally."

"Sounds good. Let's try it."

It worked and they set off at an easy canter down the track. It still hurt badly but the damage was getting no worse. Hywel could cope with that, just!

"Fine. Speed it up," he called to his companion.

They made good time to Raglan, getting there shortly after noon. The warrior stopped in a clump of trees just below the llys where they unwound Hywel's mock bonds. The warrior coiled the rope and slung it over his shoulder then grinned at Hywel.

"Keep on this track for another seven kilometres or so and you'll come a ridge which overlooks Trefynwy and the river Wye. ... Well, goodbye worm. I never did ask you your proper name."

Hywel smiled and stuck out his hand.

"What are names between friends and you've been a true friend to me. You turned what could have been a long session of agonising torture into a painful but tolerable ride. I thank you from my heart, warrior. May the gods save you from your Bear."

CHAPTER 12 – ROMAN TERRITORY

Hywel reached the outskirts of Trefynwy by mid afternoon and hesitated. He was stiff and very sore and he needed to examine his damage and to recover some strength before he continued his journey. That required food, sleep and salves - if he could find any. He wasn't sure where the next village on the other side of the river was - it might be a long way. Trefynwy was on the wrong side of the river and still in Silure territory. But there was a strong force of Romans there and he should be safe enough. He would stay.

He dug the badge of an imperial Roman messenger out of his bag and hung it on its thong round his neck under his tunic. His friend Aulus had given it to him on a previous visit and it guaranteed him free passage through any Roman checkpoint, including the one outside Aulus' office. He didn't need to use it here - the guards were friendly and relaxed. They passed him into Trefynwy with a smiling greeting and directions to a Roman inn that accepted him without argument. He collapsed on the bed they gave him and fell fast asleep immediately.

Hywel was starving hungry when he woke the next morning. He had slept as deeply as a dead man and the normal noises of the inn hadn't disturbed him at all. He had slept through supper and, by the quality of the light, he had slept through breakfast too. He tried to sit up but every bit of his body protested and refused to move. He groaned and lay back. What did he need first - food or more sleep? ... Neither - he needed to relieve himself or he would wet the bed like a baby.

He forced himself upright with the assistance of many groans and curses and dealt with his immediate needs. It was only then that he realised the full damage that the Bear had done to his private parts. Hywel was sickened and disgusted with himself but there was nothing effective that he could do without access to a proper bath and salves. He couldn't work out how he could possibly get his revenge on the Bear, much as he wanted it, and he felt a total failure.

Eventually, his hunger overcame his depression and he went in search of food. The inn was deserted but a smiling servant appeared and offered him breakfast.

"Do you have any public baths in Trefynwy?" he croaked as he made his way slowly to a table.

Aulus had introduced him to Roman baths on his second visit to Gloucester. They had warm water and attendant slaves to massage the stiffness out their customers' limbs. They were pure luxury and Hywel's soul yearned for them.

"No. There is some talk of building some here but the nearest are in Gloucester or maybe Usk."

Hywel groaned and winced as he sat down at the table.

"Any private ones?"

The servant looked at him curiously.

"Are you hurt?"

Hywel nodded.

"Yes. I met a bear in Y Fenni but it decided I was harmless and let me go after roughing me up a bit."

"Have you told the authorities?"

"Later. I need to recover first. The bath? I can pay well."

"Sorry, none that I know of. We are having some built for the inn but the workmen have only just started and it looks like being a long job. I'll bring some hot water to your room after I've brought your food."

Hywel thought hard as he ate his way through a huge meal. He did not really need to go to Lydney as he did not need to use his step-grandfather as a cover story any more. The less riding he did the better so he should make straight for Aulus - and the Gloucester baths!

Hywel twisted and turned in his seat to check his back. It still hurt but it was not nearly as stiff as it was when he woke up. His legs also worked after a fashion. If he could find a herbalist and buy some salves for his grazes he should be able to ride. He looked at the weather - cold, grey drizzle. Uggh! Maybe tomorrow was soon enough to start.

Hywel rested and tended his injuries for three days. Then he crossed the bridge and started on a long steep climb up a track that soon disappeared into the forest. According to the innkeeper, it came to a ridge, then crossed a plateau, went down an escarpment, turned left at the river Severn, and ended up in Gloucester. The innkeeper also described the small, secretive, sullen people who lived in the forest. He believed that they were descended from the slaves of the Old Ones and that they talked to evil spirits.

What he did not say was that the forest that covered the plateau was criss-crossed by a confusing maze of tracks. Hywel was sitting in a clearing, hopelessly lost, and eating his lunch when one of the innkeeper's hobgoblins appeared and nodded politely.

"Lost?" he asked in heavily accented Celtic.

"Yes. Very lost. I need to get to Gloucester. Can you help?" Hywel smiled hopefully.

"Gloucester?"

Hywel realised that he probably did not know much about the world outside the forest and he amended his request. "First I need the big river."

"Ah! The big river. Yes. That way." He turned and pointed roughly in the direction Hywel had been heading.

"Can you show me?"

The man looked at Hywel thoughtfully, nodded and let out a piercing, warbling whistle. He then sat down beside Hywel who offered to share his food. He took some cheese, smiled and thanked him.

No hobgoblin, this. Just a man who was economical with words. They sat in companionable silence for a while before a scruffy, barefooted boy appeared.

"My son," explained the man. "He will show you."

They talked together in a patois Hywel did not understand and the boy nodded twice.

"I will show you to where you can see the big river," he said slowly and carefully. "Come."

Hywel waved goodbye to his father and led his horse after the boy. It was not far and they were soon standing on a rock that gave a fantastic view of the River Severn winding its way through the flat lands that were far below them. A narrow track to the right zigzagged sharply down the incredibly steep hill.

"The big river," said the boy proudly.

"Thank you," Hywel replied gratefully and offered him a small silver coin as a reward.

The boy put his hands behind his back, stepped back sharply as though Hywel had hit him and shook his head violently.

"No! No money. Good to help," he said indignantly.

"I'm sorry. I didn't mean to insult you. ... Would you like an apple?" the boy relaxed and nodded grudgingly. Hywel gave him two and they parted amicably.

Hywel made his way down the steep and slippery track very slowly and carefully to the valley bottom. He sighed with relief as he set off on the last leg to Gloucester. It was getting late in the day now and he would have to hurry to get inside the gates before they were locked at dusk. He pounded along the Roman road that ran alongside the river but his horse was not Mellt and it soon began to tire. Hywel eased down to a canter when it became obvious that he was not going to make it in time and started to look for an inn.

He became increasingly uneasy and slowed to a walk, then to a stop. Not only was there no sign of an inn but there were no houses either. The land was flat and marshy and obviously flooded in winter so nobody lived on it. Hywel cast his mind back. There had been a small village where the track from the forest joined the Roman road but he did not remember any houses since then. The light was fading fast and he could not get back to that village before dark. Hywel swore. He would have to spend the night in the open - and if he did not get a move on, he would not be able to see to collect wood for a fire. He swore again and turned his horse towards a clump of trees on top of a small hillock. He swore many more times as he collected wood and set up camp in the lee of a large, prickly bramble bush.

Hywel felt much more cheerful once the fire was burning. His horse was grazing happily enough on sparse, stunted, salt-stained grass and it was time to feed himself. Then he remembered and swore again - he had shared most of his food with the people in the forest. He had a small chunk of bread left, a tiny piece of cheese, eight roasted acorns and ... right at the bottom of the pack, a squashed and dusty strip of smoked meat, about four centimetres by ten. He was not going to get fat on that lot! Never mind. He had been hungry before.

Hywel put another branch on the fire and wrapped his cloak around him. His injuries were all stiffening up again now that he had stopped moving. Fortunately, the drizzle had eased off and most of him was dry. He sat by the fire and decided to talk to Bard Emrys in his mind to cheer himself up.

'Greetings, Great Lord. A humble and battered apprentice requests audience.'

'Hywel!' Emrys said in surprise. *'I didn't expect to hear from you. I'm with your family.'*

Hywel nearly started to cry. How he longed to be there too.

'And I'm sitting under a tree, getting wet.'

'May I ask why you are sitting under a tree instead of in a comfortable inn?'

'I got delayed and couldn't make it into Gloucester before dark.'

'You said you were battered?'

'Yes, but don't tell my grandmother. She'd only worry. This is what happened...'

He told Emrys about his experiences in Y Fenni and there was a thoughtful pause.

'What did you say this character was called?'

'The Bear. You know I told you that the warrior from Gwent told the king that the Silures would provide the overall leader for any force we sent to help them?'

'Yes.'

'Well, if this man is suggested as that leader, tell Lord Rhys not to send any warriors at all,' Hywel said

urgently. *'He is more dangerous to them than a whole legion of Romans.'*

'All right, I'll tell him,' Emrys replied. *'But that makes it difficult for you. Obviously you can't come back through Gwent in case he catches you again so why don't you stay in Gloucester with Aulus until your father can pick you up by ship in the spring?'*

Hywel shuddered.

'I'll find a way back. I want to get home as soon as I can. I don't like this spying game one little bit. And besides, the Irish are going to attack us. I need to be with you to monitor Cathmor's mind so that we have advance warning of what the Irish intend to do. But more important still, I want to be back so that I can fight and kill Pebyn.'

Emrys laughed.

'Getting bloodthirsty in your old age! I've got to leave you now. Your grandmother sends you her love and says take care.'

CHAPTER 13 – GLOUCESTER

Hywel hurt and he was wet, cold and horribly hungry when he entered Gloucester shortly after dawn. He decided to go to an inn to sort himself out before approaching his friend Aulus. First he had a huge meal and then he set off for the public baths.

He paid the tiny entry fee to a slave sitting at the door, undressed and left his clothes in one of the storage niches set in the wall. Then he sat for a short time in the cool room, or tepidarium where the hot air gradually warmed him up for the glorious hot bath still to come. Hywel always thought that this part of the ritual was a waste of time - the hot bath in the caldarium warmed you up fast enough - but everyone else did it so he did too.

Then came the fabulous moment Hywel had been waiting for. He slid down into the hot water gingerly and closed his eyes in bliss as he lay waiting for the water to work its magic. If the Romans promised to build baths like this in Nanhyfer he would help them to invade his country any day!

He was whistling happily as he left the baths. A massage then a cold plunge had followed the long soak in hot water and he felt a new man.

Now for some fresh clothes from the trader he had used on his last visit. Hywel pushed his way through the crowds that clustered around the shops and in the marketplace. The town was bigger than ever but still dirty and incredibly noisy. Most of the shops were in front of houses built along both sides of the road that joined its two forts and the rest were stalls in the market place that was just outside the old fort. The traders were selling everything and each trader was crying his wares at the top of his voice. The customers were a mixture of people - mostly slaves, quite a few off-duty soldiers, a lot of tribes people and a couple of Romans in togas.

Hywel found the shop that he had used before which sold cloth and had some made-up clothes, both Roman and Celtic. The owner recognised him and greeted him effusively.

"Two tunics and a pair of trews? Of course, sir."

He looked at Hywel closely.

"You've grown quite a bit since last spring and filled out too. Try that tunic, just for size. ... Too small? I thought so. ... This one should be better." It was and it was loose enough for Hywel to move freely. The trews were easy, the first offering fitted well. He paid for his purchases with silver that he had taken from the hem of his cloak and walked back to the inn briskly.

Now for his friend, Aulus. A letter first, just in case his presence there embarrassed him. Hywel borrowed writing materials from the innkeeper and a boy delivered the letter while Hywel lounged in front of the fire toying with a beaker of wine. He need not have worried about Aulus. His personal slave, Lucius, arrived almost as soon as the boy got back from delivering the letter.

"Hywel! What a lovely surprise. Aulus wants to see you now, if not an hour ago. Let's pack your gear. Leave your horse. A groom will collect it later. Come on! We're in a hurry."

Hywel grinned. Lucius' enthusiasm was a tonic. Hywel had spent several holidays with Aulus and his family when he was younger and Lucius had often rescued him from the results of his own folly. They were as close as brothers and shared many interests.

He paid the innkeeper and followed Lucius who led him at a fast pace to Aulus' villa in the centre of the old fort. The sentries waved them through with broad grins and one of them muttered a greeting to Hywel under his breath. In many ways, it was just like coming home.

They went into the main room, or atrium, of the house where Aulus was pacing up and down as he waited for Hywel. He stopped pacing and looked at him solemnly.

"Hail, Hywel son of Owain," he said.

"Hail, Aulus Cornelius Calvus. May the gods protect you," Hywel replied, equally solemnly.

Formalities over, he was suddenly enveloped in a huge hug that almost swept him off his feet - which was most uncharacteristic behaviour for a general!

"Hywel! I am delighted to see you! I was bored, miserable and lonely and you appear as a gift from the gods! How did you know that I wanted to talk to you?"

Aulus was a slim, lively, intelligent man of middle height in his early forties. Hywel was concerned to see that he had aged a lot since he had last seen him - he was like a skeleton, his eyes were sunken and the hair over his ears was showing streaks of white.

"I didn't know that you did, sir," Hywel replied. "I just knew that I wanted to talk to you, so I came."

"Well, Hywel! I can not tell you how pleased I am to see you. My world is collapsing round my ears and you are a welcome sign of sanity. What brings you here?"

"The Silures. They are planning to attack you in the spring and they came to my king to get warriors to support them. There was no way we could get the message to you in time by sea so I thought that I should come overland. It's been an interesting experience."

"I am sure it has. You must tell me about it later. ... You have been a true friend, Hywel, and I will never forget you."

That was an interesting statement - 'have been' ... 'never forget' - and now he has gone all thoughtful and quiet on me, thought Hywel.

"What's wrong, sir?" he asked him gently.

"I have resigned, Hywel, and I am waiting for my replacement."

"Resigned? Completely? Or just from this post?"

"Completely - after over twenty years service to the state. It is one of the few privileges of an unhappy general. The government is in chaos; the Emperor Nero is mad and being driven out of office – he may well have gone by now; various elements of the army are intriguing to get their own generals to replace him; and the provincial governor in Britain is at loggerheads with his three legion commanders. And this selfishness is likely to cost us the empire. Do you know, Hywel, I have less than three and a half thousand soldiers to man three forts and to defend the most turbulent border in the world - and nobody cares? Perhaps I might just have been able to cope but now they are taking another thousand legionaries off me to support Vitellius in his campaign against the other imperial candidates - which will inevitably turn to all out civil war. I can hold the border by confining my troops to their forts, they are all stocked for a long siege, but I do not want to bother. I have had enough, Hywel. I want out."

Hywel was deeply saddened to see tears in his eyes.

"When is your successor likely to arrive?"

"I do not know. I sent my letter to the provincial governor about five weeks ago and he approved it, but it has to be cleared by Rome. That means about six weeks in each direction, longer if there is a civil war, and then the new man has to get here from wherever he is. So, somewhere between three and four months from now. The uncertainty is adding to my depression." He looked like a beaten dog - absolutely miserable.

Fortunately, Lucius came in at that moment, together with a servant who started laying out lunch on a table. Lucius came across the room in response to Hywel's agonised grimace for help.

"Lunch is ready, sir," he said to Aulus who was lying back listlessly in his chair. "The cook asks if you would like him to make that cheese and egg dish you enjoyed yesterday?"

Aulus shook his head wordlessly and didn't move. Lucius turned to Hywel and grinned.

"Several of your favourites are there, master Hywel."

Hywel winked at him and turned to Aulus.

"Could we eat, please, sir? I spent last night shivering and starving under a tree, dreaming of the food you would feed me today."

"You go ahead. I am not hungry."

"It's no fun eating alone, sir. Please?"

"Oh, very well."

He got up slowly and helped himself to about enough food as would keep a sparrow alive for half a day.

"Why were you sitting under a tree last night? Could you not afford an inn?"

"It's the end of a long story. Let me tell you about the warrior tests first. And, by the way, thank you for the saddle. It was great."

"Those tests are barbaric," he snapped, "and should be stopped."

"They were not half as barbaric as what happened to me on my journey, sir. I'd like to tell you about that too."

That caught his interest and after that, he became the friend Hywel knew instead of a depressed, beaten man. They talked long into the night, or at least Hywel did, and Aulus seemed relaxed and almost happy when they finally went to their beds.

Lucius and Hywel went off to their private place to talk after Aulus had gone to work the next morning. In many ways, Lucius was closer to Aulus than a son and it would be no exaggeration to say that he would die for him.

"I'm so glad you've come, Hywel," he said. "I was beginning to worry seriously about Aulus as he was starting to feel suicidal. He believes that he has wasted his life's work and, as neither his family nor his country need him any more, he may as well be dead."

"Uggh! He certainly isn't the cheerful, confident man I used to know but I hadn't realised it was that bad! What about his wife, can't she do anything?"

"She's in Rome with the rest of his family. She went in August with Marcus, his last chief of staff, who was posted to a legion in Greece. You see, the state will only provide protection, transport and accommodation for the families of serving officials and Aulus knew that, if he resigned, he would no longer be entitled to it. It wasn't the money, it was the protection that worried him, and now he's even more worried about the danger to her of civil war in Rome itself."

"So, he's lost both his family and his best friend. He must be horribly lonely," Hywel said thoughtfully, remembering his own loneliness on the journey.

"Yes, and there's more. ... The son of one of his friends is a junior tribune here and he's being stupid. He's refusing to accept that Emperor Nero is a god. Unless he changes his mind, makes a sacrifice and prays to the emperor by the end of next week, Aulus will have to order him banished from Roman territory. Then, as you know only too well, the Silures will kill him. So, in effect, Aulus will be his executioner."

"Why?" asked Hywel, horrified.

"Well, you remember the great fire in Rome when most of the city burned down?" Hywel nodded. It had happened just after his first visit to Gloucester. "Nero blamed a new sect, called Christians, for starting the fire and he killed several thousands of them in the most horrible ways. Apparently, this was a lie - they had nothing to do with the fire. The real reason was that they were exciting the mob by claiming that they had the only true god and that all the others, including Nero, were fakes. As a result, once a year all soldiers have to swear that Nero is a true god. This man won't do it."

"Not even to save his life?"

"No. Aulus and Marcus ignored the original order but this new chief of staff ..."

Lucius broke off to spit in disgust.

"He's a Nero fanatic and he held a parade to enforce it. And that's when the trouble started. The chief of staff claims that the man is disobeying an order and that makes it a disciplinary matter so now, even if he accepts Nero's divinity, he's still in deep trouble."

"And Aulus says that our customs are barbaric!" Hywel shook his head in disbelief.

"Mmmm, " agreed Lucius glumly. "How long can you stay to keep Aulus company and take his mind off his problems?"

"I had hoped to leave in the next couple of days," Hywel replied. "I can't risk getting trapped by snow on the way back. But I suppose I can wait for a week or two, but not much longer, and certainly not the three to four months he was talking about last night."

"I think he was pessimistic. The letter has been on its way already for a month and his successor could be in Britain already. That could cut it down to two."

"Sorry, Lucius, I couldn't wait for two months - not even for you. I'll wait to help him over the banishment but I leave two weeks from today."

He caught the note of decision in Hywel's voice and grinned at him wryly as he punched him on the shoulder.

"All right, great one. I give in. Tell me about your warrior tests. Were they as bad as you expected?"

They chatted happily, catching up with their news, until it was time for Lucius to supervise the preparation of Aulus' lunch. Hywel wandered out into the town. He needed time to think - deeply. He thought long and hard and reached his decision. He would become a traitor and suffer he consequences.

"Lucius," said Hywel once they were private together again, "if I tell you a serious, important secret, would you keep it?"

"Of course, under torture to the death."

"Be serious! Stop fooling."

"I was serious, Hywel. You are my friend and you are special. What is it?"

"Well, when I was 10 years old, the druids discovered that I had the ability to read and influence minds. I've worked hard on it since and concentrated on developing my range so that I could talk with my home when I was away trading. Now I can talk to certain people over very long distances and I would like to add you to that list - if you agree."

"You are crazy!" exploded Lucius. "Is it magic? "If it is, I don't want anything to do with it."

"Magic, no. It is a skill but it is rare and exceptionally secret. Let me show you. I'm coming in to your mind now."

'Hi Lucius. Relax. Don't be so twitchy. It doesn't hurt. Just think back at me.'

'Hywel?' asked Lucius diffidently.

"Yes. Not so difficult was it? You won't be able to call me but I'll call you regularly and you just need to think back at me and so we talk. Got it?"

' Yes. It's quite fun isn't it and nobody knows that we are doing it.'

'That's right. As long as you keep your face blank we are quite safe. I wish that we had done this before – it would have saved me a long and painful journey.'

'You mean that you could reach me from west Wales?'

'Yes, easily. And it will be interesting to see if I can still reach you when you get back to Rome.'

'You want me to keep this secret from everyone including Alus?'

'Particularly Alus. You see, he might think that you were a spy and a risk to any state secrets he might obtain. If he did he would have to have you killed'

'Yes, I understand. But I wouldn't do that!'

'Of course you wouldn't but he couldn't risk it while he still holds an official position. It should be different once he has left here and is on his way to Rome. You can tell him then if you like. I have similar problems myself. I would be branded a traitor if anyone found out that I'd told you and I would either be killed or expelled

from my tribe. Go and think about it. I won't do it if you don't like the idea.' Back to normal speech now, Lucius."

"Phewww! That was quite a shock, Hywel. And you look so harmless!"

"I am. You have known me for four years now and when haven't I been harmless? I haven't changed any!"

"Umm ... maybe."

"Hey, Lucius. What's the date today? I've lost track in my wanderings."

"31st October in your calendar. Why?"

"Well, tonight is one of our religious feasts when the division between this world and the Otherworld is lifted and the spirits of the dead roam abroad. I have to be particularly careful this year because I have only just become a man."

"Sounds frightening. Do you need a protector – or a woman?"

Hywel laughed.

"No thanks – certainly not a woman. I'll be fine."

"There's this nice girl, she hasn't had a man yet, and she fancies you a lot. She told me so yesterday. I can fix it for you without even trying."

"No thank you, Lucius, my life is too complicated already. ... I'm dead serious Lucius. I don't want her anywhere near me whilst I'm here."

Hywel was horrified at the thought of sleeping with a girl at Samhain; and the Bear's mauling still hurt! His initiation could wait until he got home.

Hywel examined Aulus closely at breakfast the next morning. He seemed relaxed and fairly happy so he might not bite his head off if he made his suggestion.

"Sir," he said diffidently, "I've been thinking."

"Difficult for you, Hywel?"

"Painful, sir," said Hywel with a grin. "Lucius told me yesterday about your friend's son."

His good humour vanished and he frowned heavily.

"Lucius should not have done that," he snapped. "It is nothing to do with you."

"Of course not, sir," Hywel agreed. "But isn't your friend a senator?"

"Yes. What has that to do with anything?"

Hywel took a deep breath and continued:

"Well, my old tutor said that senators could not be imprisoned or executed. They could be invited to kill themselves or they could be exiled but they couldn't be killed."

"That is true for all free Roman citizens except those in the army. The army has no civil rights so soldiers can be imprisoned, executed or exiled."

"Mmmm," Hywel said thoughtfully, "I hadn't realised that. ... But last night, sir, you said that Rome is in chaos and that the Emperor Nero will be deposed soon. When that happens, he'll no longer be a god and your friend's son won't have an oath to swear. The oath is a religious matter not a military one because he hasn't really broken any military rules."

"Only disobeying an order!"

"Yes, sir," Hywel agreed and took a deep breath. "Why not discharge him from the army - in disgrace if you like - and then exile him into my care? You couldn't have done it before I came because the locals would have slaughtered him. But I could take him home with me and look after him until it's safe for him to return to Rome."

Aulus looked at him for a long moment.

"You would do this for a man you have not even met?" he said wonderingly.

Hywel looked down at his plate and then smiled at him shyly.

"Not for him, sir, but for you. He's worrying you sick. ... and if you sent him to the Silures it would almost make you a murderer," he whispered.

Aulus turned his back to him.

"Leave me, Hywel," he said thickly.

Hywel bowed and left him. Then he sent a mind message to Lucius:

'Quick. Go to Aulus. I've just disturbed him badly. I didn't mean to. I wanted to help. But be careful. I think he's crying.'

Hywel felt like crying himself as he lay on his bed, arguing with himself until Lucius had time to talk to him.

'Why have I interfered?' thought Hywel. 'I've been so stupid! Aulus has a difficult job to do and he is bound by a discipline that I don't understand. I said that he'd be a murderer if he did his duty. Who was I to judge him?' Hywel had worked himself up into quite a state by the time Lucius came to find him.

"On your feet, Hywel. Aulus wants to see you," he said. He waited until Hywel was standing then threw his arms round him and hugged him - hard.

"They were tears of relief, idiot! He knew that it would be murder if he executed or exiled that tribune. He also knew that the chief of staff had manoeuvred him into it but he couldn't find a way out. Now you've given him one. ... Come on. Let's go and see him so that he can tell you himself."

It was frosty for the next two weeks but the sun shone and they flew past. Aulus was his old, cheerful self and they rode out together most days, sometimes hunting but mostly just exploring. Aulus started eating properly and he lost his haggard look. He announced publicly that his friend's son was to be discharged from the army and exiled beyond the border of Roman Britain but he kept the fact that he was being exiled into Hywel's custody a secret. Hywel was sure that the Silures had spies in Gloucester and a 'worm' and an ex-Roman tribune would be a very tempting target for the Bear at Y Fenni.

They talked Roman politics most evenings. Aulus was expecting, any day, to hear that the emperor Nero had been overthrown or perhaps executed.

"He is crazy, Hywel. No individual of any rank is safe from his whims and plots, so counter-plots and killings are rife. Part of the problem is that there is no obvious successor. Three contenders have strong army support and that means that they will fight for the succession, probably within Rome itself. There is one advantage to this mess though. There is no way that Rome will attack our country until we have a strong emperor in control again."

"But once you have one, the legions will come?" Hywel asked quietly.

"Yes, you are high on the list of tribes to be 'pacified'," replied Aulus.

Hywel gulped and then committed the really serious treason that he had been thinking about for so many weeks.

"Since my father and I first met you, sir, we have advocated that our tribe should seek a treaty with you, like the Brigantes. We have convinced our chief, Lord

Rhys, but he has failed to convince our king who is a fool. I went to a conference a couple of months ago, as a very junior aide. Our king accused Lord Rhys of treason and forbade him to pursue the matter further. Some of the other chiefs had mixed feelings but about half were prepared to listen...."

"Go on, Hywel," said Aulus gently, "you interest me a lot."

"I have absolutely no authority to speak of these matters and I am undoubtedly committing treason by doing so but I believe that someone in authority in Rome should know how most of my tribe feels," blurted Hywel. "There is no way that we can defeat the legions. Fight them, yes; give them a bloody nose, yes; defeat them, no way. Why waste so many lives and expose so many more to degradation and slavery when we could get an honourable treaty?"

"True."

"Do you really think that such a treaty is possible, sir?"

"Yes I do, Hywel. However, it really should be in place before the legions move into your country. Then it would be a genuine treaty instead of one forced by fright and you would get much better terms. I wish that we had negotiated it while I was still in office. The fact that we know and trust each other would have made things so much easier - even if the pen-pushers from Rome still had to make sure that the words were right."

"Could you mention it to someone suitable if the opportunity arises when you get back to Rome, sir?"

"Of course and I promise I will not say who suggested it."

CHAPTER 14 – HOMEWARD BOUND

Hywel left Gloucester for home on a bright, cloudless, frosty day. He planned to cross the Wye at Ross and to keep going northwest to the Roman fort at Clyro before turning southwest to Aberhonddu. He would be able to pick up his original route there and the detour would keep him well away from Y Fenni.

Aulus offered him an escort to Aberhonddu where the Romans had a marching camp to the west of the village but Hywel declined, as he wanted to disappear into the background again as soon as possible. Aulus was not at all happy so they compromised - he rode with Hywel to inspect Clyro and took two troops of cavalry, totalling sixty men, to protect him. The exiled tribune rode with them.

The fort at Clyro was a miniature version of the monster at Gloucester. It was built of wood on a low ridge in a bend of the river Wye and it had a fantastic view over the rich farmland of its wide valley, which was golden with the last of the autumn leaves. The view of the arc of mountains that spread across the skyline in Celtic territory to the south was equally impressive. The first snow had fallen on the highest mountains and lay on their valleys and plateaux. It had not stuck to the huge vertical faces that looked as though they had been sliced off with a sword - they shone black in the sunlight. The overall effect made Hywel think of a giant with bad teeth. He shivered, and not from the cold. The officer who commanded the fort pointed out the lowland route he would need to follow the next morning to cover the twenty kilometres to Aberhonddu.

Only then did Hywel take the exiled tribune into his confidence. He gave him the Celtic clothing he had bought for him in Gloucester and it fitted pretty well. Hywel studied him carefully.

Fortunately, his hair was black but, unfortunately, it was too short and too neatly cut for a Celt. His bright blue eyes, olive-coloured skin and erect carriage did not help either. He was clean-shaven, like most Roman soldiers, and that would be a dead give-away as almost all Celtic men had a long, drooping moustache. He would have to grow one on the journey. Hywel sighed and started plotting.

"Right. First, we need a Celtic name for you, something simple that you can pronounce - try Dewi ap Huw. Go on - say it," Hywel said encouragingly. He did. Hywel winced. It was terrible. "No. Dewwwi." His second try was better. "Dewi is your own name; ap means son of; and Huw is your father's name. Got it?" He nodded.

"But, Hywel," he protested. "I dare not open my mouth at all. Even if I just say that name people will know I'm not a Celt."

"That's right. So you keep your mouth shut and let me do the talking. And we need to hide the bottom part of your face until you have had time to grow a moustache. I think that you need a bandage across your face to conceal most of it and to give you an excuse for not talking. Let's see. … "

Hywel was exhausted by the time he had got Dewi fixed up. He left him securely hidden in the commander's quarters.

Aulus and Hywel spent a miserable evening as it was highly unlikely that they would ever see each other again. They agreed to write through a Roman trader in Gloucester but this would not be the same. Aulus gave Hywel a lengthy letter for his father and promised to deliver messages from them both to mutual friends in Rome and they went sadly to their beds.

Hywel and Dewi slipped out of the fort before dawn and waited in a copse about a kilometre away for the light to come. They then made very fast time to Aberhonddu but stopped short of the village to eat and to rest the horses. They both carried four days army marching rations and a small skin of wine. Hywel intended to sleep rough and to avoid all inns and houses until they reached the man-mountain. It would be cold, and probably wet, but contact with people was far too dangerous for Dewi.

They sat on a hill overlooking the village while Hywel pointed out the bridge and their route beyond it.

"I'll deal with anyone who stops us," said Hywel. "You keep riding at a steady pace and, whatever you do, get over that bridge. I don't want to get trapped this side of the river." Dewi nodded. "If we get separated, wait inside the forest on the left hand side of the track near that stream, the second one. I'll whistle when it's safe for you to come out but stay hidden until then." He nodded again. "Right, let's go."

Nobody took the slightest notice of them as they rode slowly through the village. There were no watchers at the bridge so the bandits who had been waiting for Hywel the last time had obviously given up and gone home. Hywel savoured the thought of what he planned to do to Pebyn when he eventually caught up with him but that would have to wait. For now, outwitting his minions was enough.

They stopped for the night earlier than Hywel wanted to. The horses were tired and they could not have got far enough past Trecastell for safety before dark. They went deep into the forest and found a sunken clearing where it was safe to light a small fire against the evening cold. Dewi unwrapped the bandage Hywel had wound around his face and spat.

"That bandage was a great disguise, Hywel, but it's horrible to wear. When can I get rid of it?"

Hywel looked at him critically and laughed. There was very little of the Roman soldier left. His hair was rumpled; his cloak and trews were badly mud stained; and he drooped with fatigue in the warmth of the fire. Another week without shaving would give him a reasonable beard.

"Sorry, you need it tomorrow until we get inside the man-mountain's house. After that, we are on friendly territory. People on the far side of his river don't know anything at all about Romans and couldn't care less if they did. They would never betray anyone who was properly sponsored."

"As I will be?" smiled Dewi

"As you will be."

"You know, Hywel, until I met you, I thought that all Celts were uncivilised barbarian savages. Tell me about your world."

"Some Celts, like some Romans, are savages - I met one recently at Y Fenni. But most people everywhere that I've been just want to be left alone to make a living - to have enough food for their family and a roof over their heads with perhaps a little left over for entertainment - pretty normal. But some of our customs are very different from yours. I'll tell you about them as we go along. ... I'm more interested in you. Lucius said that you were a tribune. Why wouldn't you worship Nero? It was only a formality wasn't it?"

Dewi smiled wryly.

"Perhaps ... but perhaps not. I don't really know."

"Go on!" Hywel urged. "Don't stop now."

"Well, ... I served a short time with the army when I was young - just long enough to qualify me to become a senator later - but I've spent the last five years in Rome studying philosophy. My teacher was fascinated by new cults, particularly those from the east, and we got to know the leaders of a cult called Christianity. One of them, Paul, was a Roman citizen who had fallen foul of the religious authorities in his homeland and had appealed to the emperor for justice. Justice was slow and he was held for a couple of years under loose house arrest that didn't stop him teaching in the temples and market places. He claimed that there was only one god and that he offered eternal life to those who believed in him. All other gods were impostors. A lot of people converted to his cult, mostly freedmen and slaves. He was a clever man and a charismatic teacher but he scared me stiff!

"I became very friendly with his scribe, a man called Luke, and we spent all our free time together. Then, the Emperor Nero claimed that the Christians started the great fire – they didn't – and he began killing large numbers of them in the most barbaric ways possible. It sickened me beyond words. As a soldier I've had to kill people - but not like that. It was foul.

"Luke and I became worried about Paul's safety and we were working on a plan to get him away from Rome when my father discovered what we were up to. To say that he was furious is the understatement of the year! We did a deal. He would keep our plan secret if I would leave Rome immediately and join the most remote army unit I could find. I left the next day without talking to Luke again. And here I am."

"Do you belong to the cult?"

"No. I found Paul's ideas interesting but not convincing. I believe that there are many wise gods. However, I cannot believe that a sadistic, crazy fiend like Nero is one of them - nobody could. There is just no way that I could swear that oath and retain my manhood. No way!"

Hywel grinned at him.

"You'll enjoy your time with us. Druid Mabon will debate philosophy with you until the cows come home - and tie you in knots too. ... Is your father still in Rome?"

"No. He couldn't bear to live there and to endure Nero's antics. He has a friend who served with him in the army here in Britain. Vespasian he's called, and he is now a very senior general in command of our large army in the Middle East. It spreads over several countries and my father has gone to help him with the diplomatic work."

"How soon do you think that it will be safe for you both to go back to Rome?"

"Not before Nero has been deposed and the new emperor, whoever he is, has a firm grip on things. Could be a couple of years. Can you put up with me for that long?"

"No problem," said Hywel airily. "Do you want us to take you back by ship? I'd like to see Rome."

"I'm not sure. That would be a tremendously long journey and I'm not a very good sailor. Perhaps Gloucester would be far enough. I've brought a set of military maps with me so I should be able to find my way back overland without too much trouble. Let's wait until Nero's gone before we start planning properly.

They continued to talk until they fell asleep.

Hywel's cloak was white with frost when he woke the next morning to the sound of Dewi stirring his iron pot on a newly lit fire.

"Wake up, Hywel, the day's half gone."

"What are you cooking?"

"Well, when we were on campaign in the army we always used to start the day with a hot drink. It set you up for the twenty five kilometre route march that followed."

"Hot water?"

"No, idiot! You warm the water a bit. Then you throw a good slug of wine in it and some herbs if you've got any. It will be ready in a minute ... now try it."

It smelled good and tasted even better. Dewi soaked his bread in it too then sucked at the hard crust like a baby before chewing and swallowing it. This was certainly a custom worth adopting, thought Hywel as he followed suit. He would speak to the master-at-arms when he got back.

They were soon on their way and passed through Trecastell without incident. Fortunately, the chatty charcoal-maker was out of sight as they cantered past his house and they reached the western edge of the forest without meeting a soul. Hywel reined in and turned to Dewi with a broad smile spread all over his face.

"We've done it! ... You're safe now! ... You can take that wretched bandage off. ... The man-mountain lives in the enclosure that lies between the two rivers. ... See it?"

"Mmm ... ," said Dewi as he unwrapped himself. "Great, Hywel! But are you sure that he won't mind me coming with you?"

"Sure I'm sure. ..." Hywel froze as he saw movement below them. Yes! It was! He switched to mind talk.

'Hey, Mellt. Hywel speaks. Come to me, boy, as fast as you can. ... Come, boy, come!' He whistled to give Mellt his position. Mellt stopped dead in his tracks. Then he turned his head towards Hywel. *"Come, boy, come!"* Then he started to gallop.

Dewi turned in alarm.

"Hywel! See that big black horse down there? He's bolting! The boy on his back can't control him."

Hywel grinned and dismounted.

"Sit still and watch."

Mellt streaked up the hill and slithered to a halt in front of Hywel. He blew into his face then pushed his head into Hywel's tunic so hard that he nearly pushed him over backwards. Hywel rubbed his nose and made a great fuss of him while he grinned at Iolo. The boy had frozen in dumbstruck amazement but the spell broke and he threw himself at Hywel from Mellt's back and hugged him tight. Dewi raised his eyebrows and sat placidly watching as the confused and excited mass of bodies swirled around him. Fortunately, the other horses were too tired to do anything except shift uneasily out of the way. Hywel finally called a halt and he and Iolo sat panting on the ground.

"I gather that you know each other," remarked Dewi as he dismounted and sat beside them.

Hywel nodded and introduced him to Iolo then switched to Celtic and repeated the introduction. Hywel frowned.

"Translating is going to be boring, people. The sooner you learn each other's language the better. Let's start now." He pointed to the man-mountain's compound. "Casa ... houses ... Tai. Repeat it." They did so.

Hywel kept it simple. "Venite! ... Come! ... Dewch!"

The man-mountain quivered in delight as Hywel called a greeting and led Dewi into his roundhouse.

"Hywel! ... Hywel, boy! It's good to see you. Are you all right? And who is this you've collected?"

"I'm fine, thank you, sir," grinned Hywel. "This is a Roman who is coming to stay with me for a bit. His proper name is unpronounceable so I'm calling him Dewi. Can we stay the night with you?"

"Stay as long as you like, boy. I want to hear all your news. A Roman, you say. I've not met one of those before. Can he speak Celtic?"

"No, not yet." Hywel turned to Dewi who had been standing politely to one side as Hywel greeted their host. "Dewi, this is Hafgan. Smile politely and stick your hand out."

The rest of that day passed very quickly. Iolo and Dewi spent most of it in the stables, admiring Mellt and learning simple words from each other. Delyth, Hafgan's eldest daughter joined them and stayed close to Iolo. The other children played round Hywel's feet while he exchanged news with Hafgan. Apparently, the two bandits they had frightened never came back and their colleagues passed through, heading west, about a week later. Apart from that, all had been peaceful and quiet.

"We had a good feast for Samhain and Iolo said all the right prayers for you."

Hywel groaned.

"I ignored it."

"The gods won't mind. Make them an extra sacrifice and say you're sorry."

"I'll do that," Hywel nodded.

It wasn't the gods that worried him - it was Bard Emrys. He had warned him to be careful. And he had given him sacred acorns. Hywel eaten them, without thinking, when he was waiting for the gates at Gloucester to open. He was in dead trouble and, if Druid Mabon ever found out ... he'd kill him! Hywel groaned again.

"Don't worry, boy. ... Come and eat."

Hafgan teased Dewi unmercifully during the meal, despite the language barrier. Dewi more than held his own. He turned out to be a pretty good conjurer for a Roman soldier and he kept the children in shrieks of laughter as he produced nuts from behind their ears and made other things disappear. Hywel played his flute for a while but they went to bed early as Hywel wanted to get away in good time the next day. He was on fire to get home now and it was only three days away if they travelled fast.

The weather the next morning was horrid - a fine drizzle and a harsh westerly wind. Camping out was going to be unpleasant. But waiting would not help and they were soon ready to leave.

The man-mountain flatly refused to accept the gold Hywel offered for his hospitality both to Iolo and to himself. He declared that they were his friends and that it had been a pleasure. However, he did agree that Hywel could give silver coins as presents to his children which made him feel much more comfortable. They left with mutual good wishes and Delyth managed to control her tears long enough to wave Iolo away.

The journey was long, wet and boring but eventually they rode up the hill out of Emlyn and caught sight the bulk of Mynydd Preseli in the distance with Carningli off to the right. Hywel was surprised at how emotional he felt. He was enormously relieved, horribly homesick and excited at the thought of sharing his news. He was also looking forward to sleeping in his own bed - he would not get up for at least a week.

"Looks good, doesn't it, Hywel," said Iolo, grinning widely. "How long do you think before we get home?"

"Twenty five kilometres and the horses are fresh - maybe three/four hours." They pushed it and clattered up to the house in the middle of the afternoon.

Hywel had sent a mind message to his grandmother and the whole family was waiting outside the house to welcome them. The three riders dismounted and Owain's groom took the horses away to the stables. Iolo turned to follow him but Hywel grabbed his arm and took him with him to greet the family. The noise was fantastic with everybody talking at once - at the top of their voices! Owain gradually restored order, banishing all the children, except Tewdwr, to Tegwyn's house, and taking the rest of the family indoors. Iolo looked extremely apprehensive until Hywel's grandmother took him quietly to one side and reassured him. After that he stayed in her shadow and sat on the floor touching her chair.

Dewi was equally apprehensive until he found that most people spoke Latin and could understand him. Hywel gave him to Tewdwr to look after and the boy glowed with pride. Then his grandmother demanded details of the journey and Hywel talked himself hoarse. They broke up into smaller groups for a feast and then continued talking late into the evening until Dewi, Iolo and Hywel were asleep on their feet.

Hywel woke very early, despite his intention to sleep for a week, and went outside to check the state of the world. Iolo was perched on the gate of the paddock watching Mellt play like a colt - rolling in the grass, waving his hooves in the air, bucking around the field on four stiff legs and, finally, charging them.

"I reckon he's glad to be back," said Iolo, fondling the horse's ears. Hywel grinned and agreed. "What are we going to do now, Hywel?" continued Iolo. "It's going to be dead boring if we don't do something."

"I agree. What do you want to do?"

"Learn to fight from horseback, go exploring, maybe chase wolves - exciting things like that."

"Would you like to go home to visit your parents?"

Iolo looked puzzled.

"Why should I want to do that? You and Mellt are my family now and my home is here."

"Until you marry Delyth and move out?"

"Until I marry Delyth," agreed Iolo solemnly.

Hywel grinned at him and punched him lightly on the shoulder.

"We'll see. I need to report back to Lord Rhys and Druid Mabon first and to find out if they have got anything planned. Want to come to the llys with me? I want to leave with Dewi and my father in a couple of hours and I'll need Mellt."

"Yes, please. I'd like that. I've never seen a high druid before, only Bard Emrys and some of the youngsters at Nanhyfer."

They reached the path to the llys when Mabon was about half way up it. They followed his tall, erect figure up the hill and the speed he climbed it belied his fifty odd years. He waited for them at the top and he was looking even more gaunt and forbidding than he normally did. His wanderings in the Otherworld during Samhain had taken a lot out of him.

He nodded to Dewi.

"You are welcome here, Roman. We need to talk. Come and see me tomorrow around noon."

He pointed his staff at Iolo and snapped: "Boy!"

"L ... Lord?" quavered Iolo shaking with terror in front of the old man.

"You have done well. You tried your best to protect your stupid master during Samhain while he did nothing to help himself."

Then it was Hywel's turn.

"You! You are a fool! Eating sacred acorns! We will have a reckoning later," he said scathingly and walked into the hall.

So, nothing had changed. Hywel still couldn't keep any secrets from him - and he still couldn't win! He winked at Iolo, who was staring open-mouthed after the druid, gave him Mellt's reins and followed Mabon.

The full council was waiting for them in the big hall. Hywel introduced Dewi to them and Lord Rhys formally made him a member of the tribe and gave him the freedom of the cantref. Then he asked Dewi to wait in another room while Hywel made his report.

The councillors listened in silence until he had finished and then they started asking detailed questions. They were most interested in his experiences at Y Fenni and also in the weakness of the Romans.

"Maybe the Silures had a point at Hwlffordd," said Bedwyr thoughtfully. "It seems that they might be able to do useful damage to the Romans, particularly if the Romans are about to lose a vastly experienced commander. What do you think, Hywel?"

"The Silures may be able to damage the countryside, sir, and quite badly. But I don't think that they will be able to tempt the Romans into the full-scale battle that would be necessary to weaken them significantly, so the loss of Aulus won't make much difference. The Roman strategy is to hold their fortresses and to let the rest go. They are already fully provisioned for a long siege."

"So," said Rhys, thoughtfully, "nothing that Hywel has discovered gives us any reason to change our own strategy - we deal with the Irish first and then consider supporting the Silures." There was a general nodding of heads around the table.

"As for the Irish," he continued, "I would like you, and the other landowners, to spend the dead months of the winter making sure that every man in the cantref knows how to use at least a spear and a bow effectively. If you can, form them into structured units that we can use to support the war bands. The master-at-arms is organising all our warriors under nominated leaders so that we can mobilise quickly when we have to."

The meeting broke up in great good humour.

"Bedwyr, Owain and Hywel .... a moment please." said Rhys. They turned back and sat beside the druid who had not moved.

"My curiosity will not wait," said Rhys with a wry grin. "I would like to have a quick word with your Roman, Hywel, about the implications of an alliance with them. Would you fetch him please?"

"Ah, Dewi," Rhys greeted him pleasantly in Latin as Hywel served him wine from a flagon a servant had left on a side table. "I am not sure if Hywel has mentioned it but I have been considering for some time the possibility of forming a formal alliance with Rome. Could you tell us what form such an alliance would take?"

Dewi looked startled.

"Yes, lord, but I am afraid that I do not know very much as I am too junior to have been involved in such negotiations. As far as I know, each treaty differs in detail but basically you agree to keep the peace, to support our army if necessary and to pay Roman taxes. How you do it within your own boundaries is entirely up to you, we do not interfere with your customs or your religious beliefs. In return, we defend you from external aggression. Your ordinary people will hardly notice any difference. Your leaders will, though. We are city dwellers by habit and we will establish a town in your territory as your capital and we would expect your leaders to live there for at least part of the year. We would build roads to link the capital with the rest of the country and some troops might be based there until we trust each other fully. We would also provide specialist engineers to help you construct buildings that no Roman town would be without – like heated baths, theatres and amphitheatres – and advice on other matters."

Dewi took a deep breath and continued:

"I am not sure what would happen over two matters – the druids and your warriors – that would be a matter of high policy and negotiation. Some tribes are exempt from taxes because they provide auxiliary soldiers for the Roman army but their loyalty then transfers to Rome and they can be deployed away from their homeland. I need to think a bit more before going further, Lord."

"Thank you Dewi, that was very helpful," replied Rhys. "Would it be possible to arrange safe conduct for a group of my councillors to visit the Brigantes? I would like to find out more about the arrangements they have with you."

"It would have been, sir, but not at the moment," said Dewi with a broad grin. "Just before I left I heard that they had revolted and that the army was going to have to sort them out. The cause of the revolt was nothing to do with us but we are involved now. Apparently, their queen decided to abandon her husband of many years and to marry his armour-bearer instead. Her husband objected forcefully so she fled to the nearest Roman troops and demanded protection. They gave it and ended up fighting her husband, almost by accident. He has now raised his whole tribe against us. It is a big tribe, spread over a wide, wild territory and it will need a serious campaign, possibly lasting years, to restore peace. So I don't think that visitors would be welcome just now."

His audience laughed.

"You are right, Dewi," said Rhys, "but we will talk about alternative sources of information another day. Thank you for your fascinating information. ... Hywel, as the nearest thing we have to an armour-bearer – you leave my wife alone or I will set your grandmother on to you! You hear me?"

"Yes, lord. I hear and I obey."

Hywel laughed at the absurdity – Rhys' wife was his grandmother's younger sister!

CHAPTER 15 – WAR PREPARATIONS

They had a lot of fun that winter and everyone in the cantref welcomed something constructive to do during the long, dark days. Most of the men were already familiar with their weapons and with the role that they would play but they were rusty after the long years of peace.

Two of Hywel's uncles, Tegwyn and Madog, shared the Carningli men between them and started training them hard. Owain made Hywel furious - he refused to give him men to command on the grounds that he was too young! They had a flaming row and he finally silenced Hywel by threatening him with three days confinement on a ship.

Dewi was equally miserable because neither Owain nor the master-at-arms would use him either, except in an advisory capacity. They rode across to see Duach and met him half way, heading towards them. His irritation with Hywel for leaving him behind on the trip to Gloucester had been replaced by a much greater irritation with his father who had also refused to give him any men. The three of them sat and plotted for a long time until they had a scheme that satisfied them.

"How are we going to sell it?" asked Duach. "There's no way that my father will listen to me at the moment. I made him furious and he used very undiplomatic language to get rid of me!"

"Mine threatened me with three days confinement on an empty ship! ... Should we try the master-at-arms?" suggested Hywel

"No. He's not here."

They thought hard but inspiration was slow to come.

"The only possibility I can think of is our sailing master, Gryffydd," Hywel said slowly. "My father listens to him. There is a problem though - they think the same way. I've never been able to use one against the other."

"Well, I can't think of anyone else. Shall we go and see him?" suggested Duach. "We've got nothing to lose."

Hywel agreed and they were soon using their persuasive powers on the big, powerful man who had taught Hywel so much about the sea and ships.

"It seems like a good idea, boys, but what's it got to do with me? I'm too old to be a warrior any more; I barely have the strength to climb on board my ship. Besides, I'm comfortable here. I don't want to see Owain again before we set sail in the spring."

Hywel grinned at the thought of him being weak and feeble - he had nearly been swept overboard in a storm earlier in the year and Gryffydd had pulled him back on board with one great heave. He finally gave in to their pleading and led the deputation to Owain.

Duach put their case as Hywel and Dewi thought it wiser to stay in the background.

"Well, you see, sir, you will need to keep a watch on every tiny bay in the cantref when the Irish are due and you don't have enough men to do that, particularly if you keep them concentrated until you know where the Irish are going to land." Owain nodded. "You do have a lot of quite sensible boys who could keep watch and act as scouts. At the moment, they are sent to a place of safety, like the fort at the top of Carningli, with the women and children and that's a terrible waste. We would like to organise and train them as watchmen and messengers to make them useful to you. Dewi knows an awful lot and he'll help us."

"What sort of age were you thinking of?" asked Owain thoughtfully.

"We hadn't decided on a fixed age bracket yet, but perhaps eight or ten to thirteen years. Anyone over that is classified as a man anyway and anyone younger might be too babyish but we could decide later."

"It seems like a good idea, Owain," rumbled Gryffydd, "and you have nothing to lose by trying it."

"You're right." replied Owain. "But, if it's to work properly, it will need to cover the whole coast, not just our bit of it." Duach and Hywel nodded enthusiastically. "Well, I'll mention it to Lord Rhys. Work on the details because he won't support a half-baked plan."

The three of them worked extremely hard on the details and they roped in Iolo, Tewdwr and Gwyn to help. The cantref already had a system of warning beacons on prominent headlands but that was fairly crude and just warned of a general threat. They devised a system of signals hung on poles that could send fairly detailed information quickly to Nanhyfer from Abergwaun in the south and Cemaes Head in the north but it needed a lot of manpower or, rather, boypower. They found it easily in the south but they had to use girlpower as well in some places to the north. They augmented the signal system with mounted messengers and the whole lot worked very well. Some of the boys wanted a more aggressive role so they let them arm themselves with bows and arrows and slings. Several of them became fine shots and riding round the cantref without the current password became a bit dangerous – even though the arrows were blunted!

Lord Rhys formed a war council and it came up with a plan that divided the coast into three - the northern cliffs, the centre that included the bay of the Afon Nyfer, and the south that included the bay of the Afon Gwaun. The centre and the south were considered to be the most vulnerable so they were commanded by Lord Pryderi and Camlach the Champion respectively and they were allocated the most men. Lord Rhys kept overall control and he also kept a large reserve under his personal command. Druid Mabon didn't really trust the new communications system and made private arrangements to send Bard Emrys to the north and Hywel to the south while he stayed at home to receive mind-messages from them.

The weather helped them a lot. There were northerly gales throughout most of January and they turned easterly for nearly all of February that gave the Irish the worst possible sea conditions. The estuary of the Afon Nyfer was sheltered from the easterly winds by the bulk of Carningli and, towards the end of February, they started to load the ships with the intention of sending them to shelter in the Afon Teifi under Gryffydd's command until the Irish had been and gone. The people who lived in the coastal strip also made provision to move their goods and furniture to safer locations and the frail and elderly moved to stay with inland relatives or friends.

Hywel monitored Cathmor's mind a couple of times a week during the winter. He discovered that the Irish chief wanted nothing to do with Lord Rhys' peace offer. The chief was also furious with Cathmor for suggesting it and he did not trust him any more. The Irish started to prepare their ships for sea in the middle of February and their warriors started to train hard.

Cathmor took a nasty fall from his horse a couple of weeks later and Hywel could not reach his mind for four days. When he recovered consciousness, he was in a lot of pain as his left leg was broken between his knee and his ankle and he was confined to his bed. Hywel reported to Lord Rhys.

"I'm sorry, lord. I don't know how much more useful information I'll be able to get out of the Irishman, Cathmor. My grandmother says that, with his leg broken where it is, he will be confined to bed for at least six weeks so it is unlikely that he will be able to take any part in the invasion. He is not likely to be involved in the planning either. But he lives close to their harbour so he will almost certainly know when they sail. I'll monitor him daily as soon as the wind goes round to the west."

"Pity to have wasted so much effort," mused Lord Rhys, "but it can not be helped. I will have to use my own judgement about when and where to deploy. Maybe it is a sign from the gods. It would have been too easy for us if we had a direct link into the Irish minds. Thank you, Hywel. Do your best."

The weather started to improve at the beginning of March. The Cemais warriors moved out to their planned positions and the warning system went onto a war footing but the foot soldiers stayed at home to look after the farms until a period of settled weather was promised. They were all as ready as they could be and most of them waited impatiently for the Irish to arrive.

The southern detachment of warriors camped around the bay of the Afon Gwaun in three groups. Camlach-the-Champion had his headquarters and his reserves (and Hywel) behind the steep-sided high ground in the centre. Nislen, Hywel's bane, held the huge sandy beach in front of Wdig Moor with a strong force of mounted warriors, and Tegwyn held the harbour of Abergwaun with a mixture of dismounted warriors and armed sailors.

Camlach insisted that the campsites, the horses and the people should stay out of sight of the sea to avoid alerting the Irish. He strengthened the two watchman positions on the cliffs on either side of the harbour and both these were manned during the hours of darkness with a warrior and three boys. They had shielded clay fire-pots with them and they would show a light if they heard or saw anything.

They waited for days and days but nothing happened. Hywel checked Cathmor's mind but he did not know very much. Boats were going in and out of Waterford harbour all the time but he took no notice of them or of the invasion preparations either. He was a dead loss.

Gryffydd decided to rely on his own instincts. He thought that the weather was promising a relatively calm patch for several days so he sailed north with all three of Owain's ships, which were captained by their mates. Lord Rhys agreed and mobilised the Cemaes foot soldiers.

Later that same day Camlach's southern group was joined by an unexpected but very welcome group of warrior reinforcements - two twenty-man warbands, one from Deugleddyf, commanded by Huw, and one from Emlyn. Camlach incorporated the bands into his reserve force and allocated them a camping area behind the tree line. Hywel, who was acting as Camlach's aide, showed them the way but, before they reached it, Cei suddenly appeared alone and grinning all over his face.

"Hi, Hywel," he called as he approached. "I've come to join you. Who do I report to?"

"You ungrammatical lout," he replied. "Camlach our Champion is in command. He's over that way somewhere. Come and find me when you've seen him."

Huw, Hywel and Cei sat just inside the trees, watching the sun setting over the sea in a blaze of orange and gold, while they caught up on their news.

Huw and Cei were both incensed by the king and it sounded as though Hywel had missed a great deal of entertainment.

"It was a farce, Hywel," said Huw. "All the warbands going to help the Silures assembled on the due date at the king's llys in Arberth. We looked good - clean, polished and raring to go. Every man had a good shield, a sword and at least one spear and their horses were fit, tough little beasts. We set up camp and waited for instructions. We waited for four days and then the instructions came - 'Go home.' - the king had changed his mind! Can you believe it?"

"You can't mean it!" Hywel gasped.

"True as I sit here. My father had come with us that far and I've never seen him so furious! He didn't want to waste our preparations so he sent me help you instead and here I am with twenty very good warriors."

"The warrior who commanded our band decided to come here too," said Cei, "and he sent a messenger to Emlyn to tell our lord what he had done. I hadn't been allowed to go to Gwent but, with this news, my lord relented and let me come here to join you. So, here I am, at your command." He grinned broadly.

"You are both extremely welcome," Hywel replied. "The only problem we have is a marked absence of anyone to fight. We've been sitting here for ages, getting more and more bored."

"But the weather was marginal until a few days ago," said Cei. "They'll need a couple of days for the crossing and the earliest they can come is tomorrow morning - more likely to be the next day."

"You could be right," Hywel said as he watched the sun vanish below the horizon. "I hope you are, as it will be a horrible anti-climax if they don't come at all."

He stirred himself and got to his feet.

"Come on. ... We need to get our supper and our beds organised now as Camlach has banned movement, noise and lights after dark. He gets us up well before dawn too, so sleep is precious. I'm really glad that you've come. Duach is stuck in Nanhyfer with our centre force and so is my new Roman friend, Dewi, so I was feeling a bit lonely."

Iolo woke Hywel in the middle of the night by putting a hand over his mouth and shaking him gently.

"They're coming!" he hissed into his ear. "I'm on watch and first we heard voices and then, just before the moon set, we saw dark shadows on the water - at least ten longboats and a much bigger shadow that could be the experimental ship. I've just told Camlach and I'm on my way back. Coming?"

Hywel had slept in his clothes so he slipped into his sandals and followed Iolo to the cliff edge. He could hear voices out to sea but he could not make out the words. They seemed to be quite relaxed - they were probably waiting for first light.

Hywel called Druid Mabon in his mind and then Bard Emrys and reported what had been seen and heard. Neither of them had any news.

The lookouts stretched their eyes and ears towards the invaders as the wind fell away and the night got blacker and blacker until it was almost impossible to see anything except a thin line of white where small waves broke on the rocks below them. They kept as quiet as mice as they lay flat on the cliff top with just their heads sticking over the edge.

Hywel could feel Iolo shivering beside him but he could not decide whether it was from cold or excitement. It certainly could not be from fright - Iolo didn't have a fearful bone in his body.

Eventually, and all too slowly, the sky to the east started to lighten and a voice on the boats snapped out a command. There were other small noises from the boats, then a laugh, and then a splashing noise. The warrior with the lookouts sent a boy to tell Camlach and Hywel went with him.

Suddenly, longboats appeared out of the darkness, moving fast towards the beach at Wdig. Hywel tried to count them and the number of warriors in each boat but it was difficult - maybe fifteen or eighteen boats with eight or ten warriors in each.

The beach was still deserted; Camlach was sticking to his plan for an ambush and discipline was holding. Hywel reported to Druid Mabon - he still had no news.

CHAPTER 16 – THE ATTACK

Hywel was very surprised that the strengthening light showed only eight longboats heading for the beach as the shadows on the water earlier had suggested that there were several more. He looked around and could just see six more heading towards the harbour.

More importantly, the experimental ship was also heading for the harbour - her sails were furled and she was being propelled by six oars on each side! He flashed the information to Druid Mabon.

The boats heading for Wdig beached on the sand and their crews lifted and dragged them up to the high-water mark. Hywel grinned with satisfaction. That was exactly what Camlach had hoped they would do. The crews then started to unload their armour and weapons.

Camlach did not blow his horn.

Hywel ran across to where he was standing with a group of the warriors who commanded the reserves, including Huw and Cei, and saw a horseman heading towards Nislen's forces at breakneck speed and another heading for the harbour. Camlach was briefing the group.

"Right then. No horn signals until that ship is tied up or anchored in the harbour - we mustn't frighten her off.

"Nislen can attack and sort out the group that has landed in front of him but he mustn't move until the ship is out of sight around the headland. Lord Huw and the Emlyn troop, please go and help him.

"Tegwyn mustn't take any action at all until the ship feels safe - he may need to withdraw some of his people out of sight in the meantime. You three - take your troops of foot soldiers to support him but keep well back and under cover until he calls for you.

"And remember, everybody, don't kill any more of the Irish than you have too - a ransom is much more useful than a dead body! May the gods keep you safe and give you glory."

The commanders grinned and went to do his bidding.

Hywel was left, feeling a bit lonely, with a small group of aides and messengers waiting for instructions. Grooms led up their horses and Iolo, leading Mellt, joined Hywel.

"What happens now?" he asked in a low voice as they mounted. "When do we get into action?"

"I don't know Iolo, but stick around and we'll find out."

He grinned and they followed Camlach across to the headland immediately overlooking the harbour where they dismounted. Camlach called Hywel to join him and they crawled to the edge of the cliff in order to stay out of sight of the ship.

"What do you think, Hywel?" Camlach asked in a whisper.

"She doesn't suspect anything yet, sir," he replied. "I think that she's planning to tie up to the jetty - there's no one anywhere near the anchor. Maybe another ten or fifteen minutes. Two men to each oar, making twenty four; there may be some more below but I doubt it - they would all be on deck to see what was happening. And look, sir! The prize! That redheaded warrior is their chief! He hates my uncle - the gods have obviously brought them together!"

"I like it!" chuckled Camlach. "Your uncle is very nearly as good a warrior as I am, although he's carrying too much weight at the moment. He'll laugh at the Irishman and get him to lose his temper before he flattens him. We'll see some pretty sword play here, Hywel, if we can get the Irishman off his ship."

"See the bulky youngster standing behind the Irish chief, sir?"

"Yes. What of him?"

"He's tried to kill me three times. Can I have him after Tegwyn's defeated the chief?"

"Yes."

They watched the ship manoeuvre to come alongside the jetty and it was certainly impressive. Hywel gave Tegwyn a running commentary in his mind and described the Irish chief in great detail. Tegwyn was in tearing spirits but extremely impatient. He said that he had ambush parties under cover in the houses around the harbour and that they had already bagged fourteen of the Irishmen off the longboats and were still collecting them.

'It's simple, Hywel. We've blocked up every chink of light in the houses so the insides are pitch dark and we've narrowed the doorways so that only one man can get in at a time. We have one of our men behind the door with a cudgel - he lets them get inside and then knocks them out. His mates catch them when they fall and tie them up and gag them. The blacksmith is having a great time - I only hope that he hasn't hit too hard and killed his victims!'

Hywel grinned to himself and wished that he could tell Camlach but he reported to Druid Mabon instead. He had no news.

The ship finally docked and the Irish chief jumped ashore with ten of the oarsmen following close behind.

He led his force inland towards the back of the harbour. The others split into two groups and headed for the buildings. Tegwyn waited until the Irish warriors were strung out alongside the harbour buildings. Then he let out a huge bellow:

"STOP!"

The Irish stopped and looked around them apprehensively as Tegwyn's warriors appeared from behind the buildings and stood with their weapons ready.

Then Tegwyn appeared. He looked magnificent. He was stripped to the waist and he had decorated his chest with mystical symbols painted in blue. His arms gleamed with gold and his torc hung heavily around his neck.

"Stop and listen to me! I am Tegwyn ap Meredith and that redheaded cockerel you call your chief has dared to threaten me. I challenge him to single combat. Let your Champion stand aside and let us see your chief's guts - if he has any!"

The Irish growled and moved forward menacingly. Their chief waved them back, screamed his war cry and launched himself at Tegwyn.

They were soon at it hammer and tongs but Tegwyn was never in any danger as his swordplay was fantastic. He toyed with the Irishman and kept goading him to attack until he was too tired to lift his sword far enough for a decent blow.

Then Tegwyn moved. He lunged at the Irishman and held the point of his sword to his throat.

"Surrender!" commanded Tegwyn.

The Irishman stood panting and he swayed with fatigue. Tegwyn pressed harder and a trickle of blood ran down into his sweaty tunic. He sank slowly to his knees, bowed his head in submission and offered his sword to Tegwyn on outstretched hands. Tegwyn took it and gestured to two of his warriors who stepped forward and took the Irish chief into custody.

"Disarm them, boys, and take them to the stockade," he called to the rest of his men and then he walked away into to village to direct operations against the remaining longboat Irish.

"Well, Hywel, he hasn't lost any of his skill, has he?" said Camlach as he stood up and stretched

"I didn't know that he was that good, sir," Hywel said admiringly. "But, please can I go now before his warriors take Pebyn?"

"Yes, but remember what I said about hostages."

Hywel ran across to Iolo who was holding Mellt and his own mount. He flung himself into the saddle and headed for the harbour at breakneck speed with Iolo in close support. As he rode, Hywel reported to Druid Mabon. He was absolutely delighted.

'Thank you Hywel. So, you have the chief, his ship and a lot of his warriors. Keep them safe and Lord Rhys and I will be with you shortly. I will bring your father with us to look at the ship. I will also get the supply wagons moving for a monster feast. We will not wait for a messenger as one has just arrived with news of the boats off shore - we will use him as the excuse.'

Hywel was in too much of a hurry to listen to Mabon's ramblings and ignored him as Mellt clattered onto the jetty. Tegwyn's warriors were busy herding the captured Irish towards the prisoners' compound but Pebyn wasn't among them. Nor was he anywhere to be seen in the village. So he had to be on the ship.

"Stay back, Iolo," said Hywel as he climbed on board. "This one's mine." The deck was empty and so were the crew's quarters. Hywel slid down a hatchway into the hold that also appeared to be empty except for a couple of piles of sacks. He tore at them and scattered them round the hold in frustration. Where was Pebyn?

He found him huddled head down in a corner under the last of the sacks. Hywel went icy cold.

"On your feet, Pebyn," he said softly. Pebyn huddled deeper into his corner. "On your feet!" Hywel commanded and poked him with his sword.

"Noooo!" he wailed.

Hywel grabbed the back of his cloak and dragged him upright.

"I said 'On your feet.' coward. Are you too scared to face me?"

His face was blubbered in tears and he nodded miserably.

"I'm going to kill you anyway, whether you fight me or not. ... Draw your sword."

Pebyn screamed and fell to the deck again. He moaned as he curled himself into a ball with his arms around his head and started rocking himself backwards and forwards.

Hywel felt totally bewildered. He could not kill a helpless, gibbering idiot. That is, if he wasn't pretending. Hywel poked him with his sword a couple of times. Pebyn was not pretending. He was truly out of his mind. Hywel felt sick as he went back on deck and breathed deeply.

"What happened?" asked Iolo who was hovering at his side.

"I'll tell you later, Iolo. Stay here, would you, and don't let anyone except Druid Mabon into the hold."

Hywel went to the end of the harbour and sat looking out to sea. He needed to think. No one except Iolo and Camlach knew that Pebyn was here. If it became public knowledge then he would have to be tried as a traitor as well as an outlaw and executed. But what point was there in that if he was out of his mind? Why not just leave it and let him go back with the Irish? He could not do anything to hurt anyone again. Hywel needed to consult Druid Mabon who was still in a good humour when Hywel called him and he agreed with his suggestion.

'Yes, Hywel. It is a good idea. Keep him under guard until we get to you. I will tell Lord Rhys.'

The remaining pockets of Irish resistance were squashed by noon and the attackers were disarmed and herded into two compounds under strong guard. The chief was kept apart in a roundhouse where four Cemaes warriors watched his every move.

The Welsh casualties had been remarkably light - no dead and only a couple of serious injuries. Two Irishmen had been killed and another four did not look as though they would make it but Llwyd, the druid doctor, was soon working on them so they might live.

Lord Rhys joined them later that afternoon, together with a large group of people including his son, Lord Pryderi and Duach. Everybody, warriors and foot soldiers alike, cheered him loudly as he rode into the camp facing the beach at Wdyg. He congratulated Camlach in front of the troops and everybody cheered again. Then he dismissed the army and went to talk to the Irish chief.

Hywel took Mabon to see Pebyn who was still huddled in a corner of the ship.

"Did you check his mind, Hywel?" Mabon asked as they looked down on the pathetic bundle.

"No, lord. I felt too sick."

"Quite right, too. Do not worry, Hywel. His state is nothing to do with you or with any action that you took. His mind was not stable, even as a child. I had hoped that he would grow out of it but, obviously, it got worse. Any real pressure would cause him to collapse as he has done. Leave everything to me. You may go."

Hywel bowed and left him.

Huw, Cei, Hywel and Duach were sitting on the shore some time later when a messenger found them and summoned them to a conference of the chiefs and war leaders who were sitting on the ground in a half circle around Lord Rhys.

"I think that everyone is here, so I'll start," he said. "Now we have defeated the Irish and their chief has agreed to terms, I want to make the following dispositions:

"Firstly, we keep their ship and I give that to Tegwyn ap Meredith for his magnificent fight."

Everyone cheered loudly.

"Secondly, we dispose of their weapons and the agreed ransom in accordance with the rules of the cantref. I wish to make the war bands of Emlyn and Deugleddyf honorary members of the cantref so that they can share equally with us."

Everyone cheered again.

"Thirdly, I wish to make a present of the Irish chief and two of his war-leaders to the king of Dyfed. I would like ten warriors from each of Emlyn and Deugleddyf to help escort them to the king. Lord Pryderi will command and they start tomorrow."

Everyone cheered again but most people missed the hidden message. The king had sworn publicly in Hwlffordd, before all his lords, that the Irish were friends and that they had no intention of invading anyone! The four boys had all been at that meeting and they had heard the king too. They started laughing uncontrollably. Lord Rhys waited for them to stop but they could not.

"If someone would please strangle the small fry, I'll continue with my last point."

They stuffed their cloaks into their mouths, pressed their faces into their arms and shook silently.

"Fourthly, I intend to let the ordinary Irish warriors take their longboats and go home. They also start tomorrow.

"That's all, gentlemen. Thank you for your efforts and enjoy your feast tonight."

Everyone cheered again and the boys let their pent up laughter explode in great whoops.

"Oh, Hywel," gasped Huw. "How exquisite! What a revenge on the king!"

"I hurt," groaned Cei. "How did he think of that? It's beautiful! I must go with that escort! I can't wait to see the king's face!"

Hywel did not have the strength to speak and tears of delight were pouring down his face. He rolled over onto his front and saw a pair of boots just in front of his nose.

"So you approve, do you, boys?" came Lord Rhys' voice, dryly, from high above his head.

They scrambled to their feet and grinned at him weakly.

"Sir," said Huw, "I speak for all of us. That was superb! Not only have you got your revenge for the

- 223 -

king's behaviour at Hwlffordd but, by including us in the escort, you have also paid back his insults to us over the Silures. I'm absolutely certain that my father will insist on commanding our part of the escort but I will fight the world to come as his deputy. Thank you so very much for all that you've done, not only for your own cantref, but for everybody else too."

Lord Rhys listened to Huw's speech with a tolerant smile on his face.

"I do not know what you mean, Huw," he said blandly. "I have only made an expensive present to my king - nothing more, and nothing less. ... Go and have a drink to celebrate your victory. .... Hywel, a moment please."

Rhys' face hardened and went blank as they moved apart; Hywel shuddered. Retribution was about to strike with a vengance!

"Hywel, did you commit treason and tell your Roman friend about our proposed treaty? And did you tell him to raise the matter with the appropriate authorities in Rome?"

"Yes, sir, but I stressed that I had no authority to do so," Hywel whispered, unable to meet his lord's eyes.

"Was that why you were so keen to see him?"

Hywel nodded miserably.

"So telling him about the Silure attack was just an excuse?"

"Yes, sir."

"Are you still in contact with him?"

Hywel felt sick. All the treason laws he had broken were coming home to roost. But he could not lie, not to this man!

"Not with the general, sir, but with his personal slave."

"Good," said Rhys with a wide smile. "Look at me boy!" he commanded. "Do you not realise what this defeat of the Irish means to you personally?"

"No sir," stammered an astounded Hywel.

"Well, it means that the king has lost so much face that he will agree to whatever I want from now on and the other chiefs will support me. So your treason was not treason after all. It was wise anticipation of my wishes. Will you please ask your friend to tell his general that Dyfed would like a formal peace treaty with them as soon as possible?" Rhys grinned at Hywel's stunned amazement. "Life is good, is it not, my brilliant young councillor?"

THE HYWEL SERIES

Spring 64AD	Hywel's Druids
Summer 64AD	Hywel's First Voyage
65AD	Hywel's Coracle
68AD	Hywel's Winter

Available from:
Abereifed Books,
Llechryd,
Cardigan,
SA43 2QN